I0615200

Morgan Dix

An Exposition of the Epistles of Saint Paul to the Galatians

and Colossians

according to the analogy of the Catholic faith

Morgan Dix

An Exposition of the Epistles of Saint Paul to the Galatians and Colossians
according to the analogy of the Catholic faith

ISBN/EAN: 9783337381554

Printed in Europe, USA, Canada, Australia, Japan

Cover: Foto ©Andreas Hilbeck / pixelio.de

More available books at **www.hansebooks.com**

AN

EXPOSITION

OF THE

EPISTLES OF SAINT PAUL

TO THE

GALATIANS AND COLOSSIANS,

ACCORDING TO THE ANALOGY OF

THE CATHOLIC FAITH.

BY

THE REV. MORGAN DIX, S. T. D.,

" Hæc et mea fides est, quando hæc est catholica fides."—S. AUGUSTINE.

NEW YORK:

PUBLISHED FOR THE AUTHOR,

AND FOR SALE AT 762 BROADWAY.

1864.

PREFACE.

A YEAR ago, the writer of the following commentaries published an Exposition of the Epistle to the Romans. The volume now offered to his brethren, has been prepared as a companion to that which preceded it. The three epistles,—to the Romans, to the Galatians, and to the Colossians,—seem to form a group, homogeneous in subject. In them, especially, are treated the theme of the Justification of the Sinner, and the theory of the Spiritual Life. They should be studied together. To feel and know the true scope of the Apostolic thought on those topics, it is not sufficient to have examined one, or even two, of them; since any one of the three is imperfect without the rest. But they should be laid side by side; and compared; and made to illustrate each other. In this consideration, the author finds the basis of his apology for the present undertaking.

The contrast is a striking one, between the inner and the outer life of the Church. Within, are peace and rest; but perpetual warfare rages around her walls. While there are afforded, in her communion, the means of grace, and the tranquil hope which comes of assured conviction, the world remains unsubdued, and the battle against error is joined from day to day. And to this is to be traced, what must appear to the casual mind an anomaly, if it do not present itself as an objection—that the history of the Church is a history of everlasting controversy. Her sons have been warriors in their time; and as many as are her saints, so many are her champions. Thus along with the preaching of the everlasting Gospel, and the ministration of the holy sacraments, there runs the strife between Light and Darkness, incessant and implacable, yet tending steadily towards triumph for the right and the true. It is an anomaly indeed: that the array of war should be thus encircling the Kingdom of Peace; that the soul should have rest in the Church, and yet that on the side where lies the enemy there should be seen, not peace, but a sword.

The controversies to which we refer may be traced through her entire history. At the same time it is possible roughly to classify them; and it will be found that in the earlier ages the struggle was for the preservation of Objective truth, while in later days Subjective applications have formed the topics of contention. Objectively, it is the mission of the Church to keep the Faith; to propagate it; to defend it. The first controversies grew out of the fulfilment of this primary duty: men had to do long and heavy battle for the creed. That great campaign, which lasted through the age of the General Councils, terminated in securing the ends for which it was prolonged; and since its triumphant close, the Nicene—or, as it has been called from the greatest of her champions, the Athanasian—faith has remained, substantially, the faith of Christians throughout the whole earth. But again: it is the mission of the Church to apply subjectively the dogmas intrusted to her care, so as to make them effectual to the salvation of the individual soul. Deeply is it to be regretted that there should ever have arisen a necessity for making this process the subject of what may be termed philosophic investigation and scientific study. Yet that necessity did, in time, arise; when some had pushed to an extreme the claim of creature-merit, and others had denied the absolute need of the grace of God, and more remained confused about the relative offices of faith, and of the works of righteousness. On these purely subjective themes have the later controversies for the most part turned. They came to a head in the 16th century, and to some extent they are still going on. Yet the Truth gains ground. The Solifidian and Antinomian hordes have been driven back: the extreme Tridentine views, together with the Lutheran scheme of justification, have alike yielded to the pressure; while those principles which, in their historical aspect, seem to be truly Catholic, have steadily risen towards the place of influence and command.

But long after the wings of an army have been routed, and its centre has been pierced, its fragments, though in flight, may spread alarm abroad, and scatter confusion along the way of retreat. The extreme theories which were pressed so warmly, when the cycle of the later contentions began, have indeed been weighed in the balance and found wanting; yet this has not prevented mischief from ensuing as the result of their former announcement. A carcass, though dead, may be dangerous from its very exhalations; and a theory, though as to its formal statement abandoned, may work invisibly for evil, notwithstanding its disgrace. It is so with the subjective theories, now exploded, to which allusion has been made. The man who would refuse to hear them, if scientifically presented, may yet unconsciously be swayed by that which he rejects. The lover of the truth must watch with care the motions of its defeated opponents; since even in the final efforts of despair there lies strange power for mischief; and falsehood may haply slay in its death, more than it slew while yet alive.

It is not necessary to recapitulate the principles on which the following commentary is based; for that would be but to repeat what was said in the preface to the Exposition of the Epistle to the Romans. But they are held as matured convictions; and the materials with which they are now to be enforced have been gathered at intervals during the past ten years. The attention of the humble-minded reader is directed in particular to the epistle to the Colossians, in the belief, that the view of the theory and method of the spiritual life there taken is directly the reverse of that which modern Protestant sects continue to advance as the only evangelical one. The writer has aimed at exhibiting that contrast as forcibly as he could. Yet, if the task has not been accomplished to the satisfaction of the reader, let him close this volume, and take the original once more, and read, and revolve, and think it out for himself, as the writer has done; and surely he must at length see the truth. That epistle is but an expansion of this thought—that the life of the child of God begins in the reception of Sacramental grace, and that his work and duty are to preserve the divine gift instrumentally conveyed to him in baptism. It will be found impossible to accommodate this epistle, satisfactorily, to the modern scheme which substitutes a late moral conversion for an early spiritual change; and he who, in a candid temper, shall have regarded, not separate expressions culled here and there by the hand of self-will, but the whole drift and course of the thought, must remain convinced that this is so. The writer may indeed have failed to make that clear to others which to himself seems clearer than the day : but, while he is ready to lay that failure at the door of his incompetency, he would urge and affirm that the view which he has taken of the Apostle's meaning is, notwithstanding, correct.

The space is vast between the wisdom of God and the inventions of men. Let us regard the holy oracles, as intended to reveal to us His modes of operation, all transcendent and divine, and all at once beyond our comprehension, and open to our loving faith; and not as though they had been given to aid us in building up some frail structure of human thoughts and opinions. We must search the Scriptures, in order to find what ought to be believed, not to discover what we believe ourselves; and we must reverence them as containing dogmas necessary and apt for all sorts and conditions of men, accounting it profanity to apply them with a view to lend authority to individual theories and private conceits. There is nothing sectarian in the word of God; and the attempt to expound it from a sectarian stand-point must result in failure. Its sound is gone out into all lands, and its words unto the ends of the world; wherefore, the nations of the redeemed must have their voice on all questions of its interpretation. It was given, not to one race, not to one age; not to the East, nor yet to the West; but to all men, everywhere, even unto the end of the world: and, therefore, it must be read and understood with reference to that common right of possession. It is the sacred trust of the Universal Church of Christ; and the voice of that Catholic body is the living witness to its meaning.

NEW YORK, July, 1863.

The Epistle

To the Galatians.

EXPOSITION

OF THE

EPISTLE TO THE GALATIANS.

INTRODUCTORY REMARKS.

THE seed of Divine Truth, called by our Blessed Lord the Word of the Kingdom, must fall, as He said in His parable, on diverse soils. In some places, it keeps its hold and brings forth abundant fruit; but in others, its fate is to be choked by tares and thorns. While we consider these results, with their modifications, we ought to take to ourselves a lesson from what we see: for the heart of the sinner is in reality the ground wherein the seed is sown; and, according to the temper and spirit of that inner man, the heavenly germ shall flourish or fail. In this connection, the letter of S. Paul to the Galatians may be held up as a mirror to the soul.

For in that Epistle we perceive how soon and how completely the precious seed, though planted by Apostolic hands, may become overlaid and stifled by adverse influences. The frivolity and unreflecting waywardness of an impulsive, capricious, and unsteady people, imperilled the Sacred Tradition almost immediately after it had been confided to them; and they who had received the Word with gladness, did yet, in time of temptation, suddenly fall away. The Sun was no sooner risen, with a burning heat of trial, and a glare of false and deceitful light, but they were scorched, and having no root, they withered: the flower fell, and the grace of the fashion of it did perish; or would have done so, but for the interposition of the Lord's own Apostle, recalling them to reason and to truth, and bidding them consider their ways and turn and be saved from the burning.

At a period long preceding that of the dawn of European civilization, there passed over from the old and legendary East, towards the shores of the Western Ocean, that branch of the

Indo-European family of nations known as the Celts or Gaels.
They migrated, as directed by the providence of Almighty God,
and spread their encampments through that part of Europe
formerly called Gallia, or Gaul, and now occupied by the French
nation. But scarcely had these wanderers arrived there, when
they began, uneasily, to push in other directions, as though dis-
satisfied and restless, and ever seeking novelty and change. The
character of the race is strongly marked : vivacity, activity, life ;
quickness in coming to decisions, instability in purpose, incon-
stancy of temper and disposition ; a passionate desire of adven-
ture, and a devotion to arms and to the art of war. Such were
the characteristics of the Gallic race. Obedient to the laws of
their nature, they wandered here and there, prying into the places
of other nations, and seeking whatever seemed desirable, by the
argument of the sword and the path of conquest. We find them,
first, in Northern Italy ; then in Macedonia ; in Thrace and
Greece ; and even at last, returning on their steps, in Asia Minor.
Somewhere about the year 380 b. c., an army of them, under
Brennus, poured down into the peninsula of Italy, and, before
they finished their campaign, took by storm and sacked the
city of Rome. Later, about 280 b. c., another host of these
restless warriors, under another and scarcely less formidable
Brennus, invaded Greece and Macedonia. It is to this armed
immigration that we must particularly direct our eyes ; for, although the main body met with divers fortunes, and at length,
near Delphi, with a disastrous overthrow, b. c. 279, yet a portion
of them,—a wing, as it were,—detaching itself from the grand
army, crossed over the Hellespont, and, finding there a fruitful
and attractive region, lying between Bithynia and Paphlagonia
on the north, Pontus on the east, and Cappadocia and Phrygia
on the south and west, plunged into it with impetuous onset, and
established itself there as in a place of permanent abode. There
were already Greek colonists in the land ; and with them the new-
comers mingled. From this conjunction the dominant race received the name of Gallo-Græci, or Gallic-Greeks ; the country
was called Gallo-Græcia ; and this was the Galatia in which,
about the year of our Lord 50, the Apostle Paul preached the
Gospel of the Lord Jesus Christ.

The Galatians would seem, from what can be gathered from
ancient writers, to have retained the characteristics of the double
fountain of their lineage ; for they had the intellectual activity of
the Greeks, together with the vivacity, the impulsiveness, and the
fickleness of the Gauls. Callimachus speaks of them as a foolish,
or unsteady and inconstant people ; and the great Saint Hilary of
Poictiers, himself one of the same family of nations, acknowledges

their trying and unteachable character. In these distinctive qualities of temper and disposition may be traced the secret of the early corruption of the Church at Galatia ; a corruption, not like that displayed at vicious and sensual Corinth, but that perversion of the intellectual apprehension, and of the theological sense, which ensues whenever men, leaving the standard of the Faith, and thinking lightly of authority, heap to themselves teachers, and follow after the speculations of self-constituted ministers whom the Lord hath not sent.

It was in or about the year 50 that S. Paul visited the region called Galatia, and preached therein the Gospel of Christ. Departing thence, he left to its uncertain fate the precious seed which he had sown in that part of the field. But presently came the Evil One, and the Enemy, to catch away the Word of life. He came in the persons of certain Judaizing teachers ; who, taking occasion from the circumstance that among the Galatian Christians there were many converts from the Jews' religion, sought to reimpose that religion as of obligation ; to recall to the practice of the rites and customs of the Mosaic law those who had discontinued such observances upon embracing the truth as it is in Jesus ; and to establish its necessity even in the case of those who had never been within the pale of the Mosaic covenant. These men, finding in the teachings and still reverenced memory of the Great Apostle, the principal barrier to success, were compelled to invent methods of undermining his authority, and of reducing to less favorable consideration, if not of bringing into positive contempt, the principles inculcated by him. They, therefore, assailed him on these two grounds : 1st, that he was not an Apostle in the full sense in which the Twelve had been such, but that his commission, whatever it was, had not a higher than mere human authority ; and, 2dly, that he, who had been appointed by the other Apostles, or some of them, as a subordinate, had not observed their teachings, nor fulfilled the obligations under which he stood to them—to deliver, viz., what they had given him in charge.

The Galatians, fickle and unsteady, had evidently been led away by these new lights ; they had compromised themselves deeply in regard to the faith ; it would seem as though they had been bewitched by these emissaries of Satan, and led to the verge of apostasy.

The Apostle, therefore, having heard of these inroads, and of this sad decline from the purity and vigor of their early faith and love, addresses to the "foolish Galatians" that strong, clear, and emphatic letter which we are about to study. He commences it with a vindication of himself ; asserting that his commission

was given him direct from God; and he further declares, that, so
far from having been instructed by the Apostles who were before
him, he had even held no intercourse with them at all for years
after his conversion. He then proceeds to argue against the
attempted revival of the Mosaic system; and for that purpose
asserts the cardinal doctrine of Justification before God, not by
the works of the Jewish Law, but through the sole merit of the
Lord Jesus Christ. He shows that the character of the former
dispensation was symbolic and analogical, proving it to have been
transient in its nature and temporary in its duration. He sets
forth, in full, the Christian system as one rich in spiritual efficacy
and in the powers of the Holy Ghost and of the world to come
These are the leading themes of this Epistle; which may be
regarded as a vindication of the Catholic faith, and of himself,
its strenuous assertor.

The Epistle to the Galatians is generally associated in thought
with that to the Romans; and, indeed, there is reason for this
connection between them. For in each, the great question is discussed, of the Justification of the Sinner before God. In one
important respect, however, they differ; that the Epistle to the
Romans is broader in its scope than that to the Galatians: for
in the former, the Apostle argues against Gentiles as well as Jews,
while in the latter it is Jewish error which he more particularly
has in view. In the Epistle to the Romans, he shows, that man
is justified, not by obedience to the Mosaic Law, as the Jews
fondly asserted, nor yet by the works of the Moral Law, as Gentiles might have inclined to hope; while, in the Epistle to the
Galatians, he addresses and refutes those only who would make
of the Mosaic System a cause of Justification. In the former he
rejects the works, as well of Nature as of the Law; while in the
latter he shows the worthlessness of those of the Law alone.

Our first general observation on this Epistle is, therefore, this:
That, when the holy Apostle speaks of the Law, he means the
Mosaic Covenant, the Jewish System; and that when he exposes
the impossibility of being justified by the works of the Law, he
intends to show these two facts: 1st, that the System of which
Moses was the commissioned founder and head, was not available
for the sinner's justification apart from Christ and from the righteousness of faith; and, 2dly, that, Christ having come, it was no
longer necessary to any man's acceptance with Almighty God.

It does not appear that, in any place in this Epistle, the word
"Law" is to be otherwise understood than as a name descriptive
of the System of the Jews' Religion.

The Epistle is divisible, readily and naturally, into three portions or sections, each consisting of two chapters.

In Chaps. I. and II., the Apostle applies himself to a personal vindication, rendered necessary by the attacks of his enemies. In this part of the Epistle, he shows that he had a true commission from the Lord ; that his doctrine was not one of human devising, but that it had been divinely communicated to him from above ; that as to practice and teaching, he had been in full accordance, all along, with the rest of the Apostles ; and that he had been perfectly consistent in his course towards those who would pervert the Gospel of Christ.

In Chaps. III. and IV., the Apostle shows, by a variety of arguments, taken from divers sources, that the Mosaic System has forever passed away, as to any obligation on any class of men ; that it was transitory in its character ; that it was but a preparation for the Gospel ; that the Gospel is, in every point of view, its superior. He likewise depicts the fatal consequences which ensue, where men, abandoning that Gospel, return, in quest of justification, to the old and lifeless form of a past age.

In Chaps. V. and VI., he presents practical results, in showing the condition of men under the dispensation of the Holy Spirit ; the true power of the Gospel ; the order of the Christian life ; and he adds such charges and injunctions as seemed to him most needed by persons in their position.

The Epistle, therefore, may be studied in three sections :

Of which Section I. contains a Personal Vindication ;

Section II. contains a Theological Argument of Salvation ;

And Section III. offers Practical Applications in respect to the Christian Life.

COMMENTARY.

THE first and second chapters of the Epistle may be regarded, as has been already remarked, as forming a section by themselves. They have a personal character, and contain, chiefly, the Apostle's vindication of his commission, his teachings, and his actions. There is but little in them of a distinctively theological nature.

The Judaizing teachers had assailed him on these grounds: That he was not an Apostle of Christ, but a disciple of the other Apostles; that he had derived from them all his knowledge of the Christian system; but that he had not observed their instructions; that he had dissembled in his conduct, in some places denying the necessity of circumcision and other matters of the ancient Law, and yet, in others, practising the things which elsewhere he had condemned. In reply to these and similar accusations, the Apostle declares, in these first chapters:—That his Apostleship was not from man, but from the Lord Jesus Christ; that he had not been indebted to men for his knowledge of the faith which he preached, because, previously to his conversion, he had been a furious assailant of the Catholic Religion, while subsequently thereto he had, for years, met with no one of the Apostles from whom to learn; that when at length he met with them at Jerusalem, they were satisfied with the substance of his preaching, as in accordance with the tradition with which they had been intrusted; and that, so far from having been guilty of inconsistencies, he had reproved them in others, even in the most eminent of the original Twelve. This is, briefly, the substance of the first and second chapters. Let us now proceed to an accurate survey and examination of the Sacred Text.

1. Paul, an apostle, (not of men, neither by man, but by Jesus Christ, and God the Father, who raised him from the dead;)

"Not of men." Not instituted or ordained by men, according to their choice or pleasure.

"Neither by man." Nor by men acting under authority from God to ordain or consecrate him to that office and ministry.

"But by Jesus Christ." By the Lord himself, directly and without human interposition or instrumentality; and as a further distinction, not by the Lord on earth, but by the Lord reigning and triumphant in Heaven, seated at the Right Hand of the Father and in the Majesty on high.

2. And all the brethren which are with me, unto the churches of Galatia:

In this introduction, it should be noted that S. Paul deviates entirely from his usual practice: in his other Epistles to the churches, he generally mentions himself alone, or himself with one other, or himself with two; he addresses some particular church or congregation of the faithful; he adds, in so addressing, some word of honor, such as "sanctified," "beloved," "called," or the like. While here he names the whole multitude of the brethren who were with him; he addresses all the churches of that region; and he adds no honorable epithet or title whatsoever. These peculiarities have been thus explained: the first, inasmuch as he would show that his action was not that of a single individual, but that it had the sanction and concurrence of the brethren at large; the second, inasmuch as the whole Church throughout that region was corrupted; and the third, because their doctrinal errors had destroyed among them the spirit of charity, and separated them from the happy interchange of Christian greetings.

▲ 3. Grace *be* to you and peace from God the Father, and *from* our Lord Jesus Christ,

3. Yet does not the Apostle withhold even from these lapsers the Apostolic benediction: that is denied to the excommunicate alone. This blessing comprises all spiritual good; for grace is the beginning of the spiritual life; and peace is its conclusion and its end: the extremes therefore being named, all intervening parts and degrees are comprehended. Grace is the source of our goodness and righteousness, and peace is the quiet repose of the mind in the Faith: the latter we enjoy as being made partakers of the former.

4. Who gave himself for our sins, that he might deliver us from this present evil world, according to the will of God and our Father:

5. To whom *be* glory for ever and ever. Amen.

6. I marvel that ye are so soon removed from him that called you into the grace of Christ unto another gospel:

4. Since the Apostle will set forth Christ as the sinner's only hope, he declares His work, when first he mentions His name.

"This present evil world:" that is, the corruption which is in the world. Not that the world is, in itself, evil; but that it is the scene and stage whereon evil is wrought by wicked and fallen man.

6. "I marvel." I am filled with wonder and amazement. And well indeed he might be. The holy Apostle expresses his astonishment at three things in particular: 1st, that they had apostatized from his teachings; 2dly, that they had done this so soon; 3dly, that they had adopted another system in the place of that which they had embraced, as he presumed, devoutly, thankfully, and under full conviction of its sufficiency and obligation. "Removed! so soon! and to another gospel!" Three grounds for horror and amazement at their fickleness, their levity, their want of faith.

"Removed from Him," &c.: *i. e.*, from Almighty GOD. For to depart from the communion and fellowship of the Apostles is to withdraw from GOD. The expression shows the shocking character of their sin. And yet it was a sin of intellect; its essence was intellectual self-will; the forsaking the Church, her Ministry, her Ordinances, her Creed, her forms, and seeking unto leaders after a man's own heart; this is the perilous downfall of the soul.

7. Which is not another; but there be some that trouble you, and would pervert the gospel of Christ.

7. "Not another"... for there cannot be two Gospels, as there cannot be two Churches, each true, or two baptisms, or two valid but different ministerial lines.

"Some that trouble you," &c. Here is the accurate description of heretics and separatists of all time, early and late: they trouble the Church and subvert the system established in the world by Christ and his Apostles. And the Judaizing teachers to whom the Apostle refers, were indeed subverters of the plans of GOD as far as lay in their power. For they would have brought men back to the obedience of the Law. But the Law was a figure and

2

a shadow; while the Gospel was the reality and the signified substance. Now, when the substance had come, and when the shadow, waxing old, had vanished away, they would have had the shadow back, and would have made of the living truth a dead and eviscerated corpse. Thus does the Pride and Intellectual Lust of Man try everlastingly to turn back the steady flow of the vast counsels of God; but in vain.

8. But though we, or an angel from heaven, preach any other gospel unto you than that which we have preached unto you, let him be accursed.

9. As we said before, so say I now again, If any *man* preach any other gospel unto you than that ye have received, let him be accursed.

8, 9. An awful anathema; but tempered with mildness. For the Apostle neither names nor directly curses any one of the offenders. At the same time, he shows that no one, not even a Peter, or a James, or any of those whom his enemies affected to reverence and admire, should be for an instant tolerated, if preaching aught contrary to or aside from the Catholic Faith. Nor does he except himself; for he protests that aught of his own which he might, independently, deliver, should be held, *ipso facto*, false and worthy of rejection.

Hence arose the canon of faith, followed by the holy Fathers and by the Councils of the Church; that if any new dogma or doctrine arise, in any quarter, it be examined with care, whether it agree with the ancient and received faith of the Catholic Church; and that if it be found repugnant to the Venerable and Apostolic Tradition as contained and expressed in the Holy Scriptures, or not in harmony therewith, it be counted heretical and pronounced "Anathema."

And, therefore, since Christ, who is the Truth, hath spoken unto us the Word of God; and since the Apostles have declared unto us the Words of Christ; if any man hold or teach aught contrary to that preaching of the Apostles, and that Word as spoken by Christ, let him be counted Anathema of all faithful people, if they would follow the mind of Saint Paul.

10. For do I now persuade men, or God? or do I seek to please men? for if I yet pleas-

10. The introduction of this verse is elliptical: we must supply something to make it clear. Having uttered his Anathema, the Apostle would

ed men, I should not be seem to have bethought himself of the servant of Christ. those Pseudo-apostles, and of their indignation and excitement at this denunciation. He, therefore, goes on to say, that he cares not how they may take it, nor what they may say; he fears them not, nor does he desire to conciliate them. It is his business to speak the truth; to reprove, with all boldness; to rebuke them that sin, before all, that others also may fear. And he declares, that in what he had just said, he had sought only to please his Master. He was pleading his cause, not before men, but before GOD: he was seeking how he might please, not men, but GOD. If it were not so, it had been easy for him to have enjoyed human applause and worldly comfort, by merely remaining what he had been before, instead of embracing the Gospel.

That may be true which has been remarked on this passage, that, at that time the Jews enjoyed, under the Roman laws and edicts, an immunity from certain prosecutions to which the Christians were exposed. The Jewish Religion was recognized by the Imperial Government; but the Christian Faith was new, and unknown, and therefore its profession was perilous. The path of safety lay therefore in that direction where the Judaizers were walking: and if the Apostle had sought either to provide for his own security, or to please other men who shrunk from persecution and distress, he should have remained, outwardly, an observer of the Mosaic Law. But this he had not done: his enemies were they who were really selfish; they were men-pleasers, but he sought to please, not men, but GOD.

11. But I certify you, brethren, that the gospel which was preached of me is not after man. 11. He returns to the statement of his opening clause, "An Apostle, not of men, neither by man." The further declaration and proof of this will be found to occupy the rest of this chapter.

"Not after man ..." not human in its origin, not human in its character.

12. For I neither received it of man, neither was I taught it, but by the revelation of Jesus Christ. 12. He neither received it from the tradition of any individual, nor was he taught it by any professed instructor.

13. For ye have heard of my conversation in time past in the Jews' 13. "Ye have heard ..." The fame of Saul's conversion, or apostacy, as the Jews called it, had spread not

religion, how that beyond measure I persecuted the church of God, and wasted it: merely to Galatia, but even to Rome itself: he mentioned to them no new things, but facts with which they were familiar.

He arranges his proof that he was an Apostle not of man or by men, as it were chronologically, according to the time before his conversion to Christianity, and that which had subsequently elapsed: he shows that the supposed instruction and teaching could not have taken place during the former term, since he was then a furious opposer of the Religion of Christ; and that no time had since occurred in which it could have been imparted. Let us first consider what he says of his former position. So far

14. And profited in the Jews' religion above many my equals in mine own nation, being more exceedingly zealous of the traditions of my fathers.

from having been a disciple of the Apostles, he had been remarkable among his own people for three things: 1st, for the excessive acrimony with which he persecuted the Church; 2dly, for an unusual and extraordinary proficiency in the

knowledge, study, and practice of the Jewish Faith and System; 3dly, for an ardent and almost extravagant zeal in attachment to every distinctive custom of his ancestral religion. And, therefore, no one who knew that history could for one instant imagine that he had learned the Gospel before the time of his formally embracing it.

15. But when it pleased God, who separated me from my mother's womb, and called me by his grace,

16. To reveal his Son in me, that I might preach him among the heathen; immediately I conferred not with flesh and blood:

15. He now proceeds to speak of the second period of his life, that following his conversion; and to vindicate himself, there also, from the charge of having been, not a duly commissioned Apostle, but a mere disciple or scholar of the Apostles.

16. "To reveal," &c. The fathers have differed as to the time when this revelation was made, some supposing that it was on the highway near Damascus, at the moment when the Lord appeared in glory; others that it was during the days and nights of darkness which immediately followed; but others, with more probability, that it was after he had been baptized by Ananias.

"I conferred not . . ." i. e. did not go for advice, for

counsel, for instruction, to "flesh and blood," *i. e.* to any human being.

17. Neither went I up to Jerusalem to them which were apostles before me; but I went into Arabia, and returned again unto Damascus.

17. Nor did he go to Jerusalem, as he might have done; where Peter, James, and John were at that time accessible : in a word, he needed no human teacher, and availed himself of none.

"Arabia . . . . Damascus." The Apostle does not say for what purpose he went into Arabia, nor on what errand he returned to Damascus, but there can be scarce a doubt that in both places he was busy in preaching the Gospel, and fulfilling his Apostleship: this seems to follow from the " immediately" of the preceding verse. And on this supposition there is greater force in the whole argument.

18. Then after three years I went up to Jerusalem to see Peter, and abode with him fifteen days.

18. Then, after three years so employed, he went up to Jerusalem, not with a view to obtaining instruction, but that he might pay due respect to Peter, the chief of the Apostles. And he remained there only a fortnight ; too short a time, if he had gone, as an ignorant man, to learn the Gospel.

19. But other of the apostles saw I none, save James the Lord's brother.

19. " Other of the Apostles . . ." Probably because they were absent at the time, engaged in the work of preaching the Gospel.

"The Lord's brother :" *i. e.* His relative and connection. This James was the son of Mary, the wife of Cleopas, sister to Saint Mary, the Virgin. That the Mother of our Lord remained Ever-virgin, is not less evidently the instinctive belief of the heart, than it is the common and assured conviction of the Church. Yet not less clear is it, that there can be no profitable disputation on the sacred theme. Indeed it were useless to argue with one by whom the contrary thought could be deliberately dwelt upon. The very haste with which we repel that thought as repugnant and shocking, not to say revolting and monstrous, implies a total want of sympathy, in that behalf, with any one to whom it should not present itself in the same light. There are subjects on which a man may feel so deeply that he shrinks from hearing them opened as topics of discussion ; and the tenet of the Perfect and Perpetual Virginity of the Blessed Mother of our

Lord, is one of these. Little is said of her in the Scriptures; many excellent things, however, are spoken of her in the heart of "all but adoring love." She appears to us, veiled in a holy and impressive mystery; and we may say of her, when men speak reproachfully, "Thou shalt hide her privily by Thine own Presence from the provoking of all men; Thou shalt keep her secretly in Thy tabernacle from the strife of tongues."

20. Now the things which I write unto you, behold, before God, I lie not.

20. This strong affirmation is intended to establish the foregoing statement of facts, as on that depended the vindication of himself as an Apostle, not of man, but of the Lord Jesus Christ.

21. Afterwards I came into the regions of Syria and Cilicia;

21. As much as to say, that he went not into Judæa, nor into any region, town, or colony thereof.

22. And was unknown by face unto the churches of Judæa which were in Christ:

22. And so far from having learned among the Jews the doctrine which he preached, he was not even known to them by face.

23. But they had heard only, That he which persecuted us in times past now preacheth the faith which once he destroyed.

24. And they glorified God in me.

23. They had heard of him, on the contrary, as an able and successful Apostle and Evangelist, and (24.) gave God glory for the powers and virtues which were manifested through him.

Let this chapter be closed with one additional observation. If, from the tone of the Apostle's words throughout it, any one should judge that he was arrogantly boasting of his independence of other men, such an opinion should immediately be revised, as it must proceed from misconception of the case. For the holy Apostle is as far from being like those proud and haughty scorners, who despise authority and speak evil of dignities, as light is dissimilar from darkness. This is a defence of himself. The things which had been asserted of him, were false; and in setting forth the truth, he has stated facts just as they were. His design is not to exalt himself; not to depreciate others; but simply to show how untrue were the words of those men, who, in reviling him, had been assailing the Church and Christ.

And again: since the Apostle so carefully declares the origin of his mission, and is so scrupulously punctual in

clearing his ministerial character from any shade of sus-
picion as to its legitimacy; let every one who desires to
receive Holy Orders, or who already has had them conferred upon him, be close in examination of the lawfulness
of his commission. The Apostolic Succession is the Spinal
Column of the Body of the Visible Church; and except
through that there can be no organic connexion with the
general system. At the beginning, Christ, our Lord,
did, with his own voice and word of mouth, and without human interposition, ordain and send a Paul; but it
is so no longer, and such a case affords no precedent suitable for common application. The sciolist and heresiarch
who should put forward such claims to-day, would be
worthy of pity and concern, but not of respectful attention.

(CHAPTER II.)

The object of the holy Apostle, in this chapter, would
seem to be, to defend himself from the second of those
charges brought by his malignant enemies. From the ac-
cusation, that he was only a disciple of the Apostles, he has
already sufficiently cleared himself. To the further accu-
sation, that he had departed from the doctrinal scheme of
the Apostles, teaching a system and principles inconsistent with those which they had taught, he now proceeds to
reply. (Accordingly, he states, in this chapter, that when
he for the second time visited Jerusalem, he took that
opportunity to present to the Apostles who were there a
formal statement of his doctrines and his practice; that
they were fully satisfied with the one, and found no ground
of complaint of the other ; and that they accordingly gave
him the right hand of fellowship, and bade him God-speed.
He then mentions certain circumstances which occurred
at Antioch, showing that, in his assertions respecting the
non-obligation of the Mosaic Law, he had used no dissimulation, but had boldly reproved those who would
have again imposed it on Christians. And he concludes
with some remarks upon the monstrous nature of such
attempts, displaying the absurd consequences which would
follow logically, if they were to be admitted and en-
couraged in the Church.

1. Then fourteen years after I went up again to Jerusalem with Barnabas, and took Titus with *me* also.

1. "Fourteen years . . . ." during which he had been constantly preaching the Gospel.

"After . . ." Either, after the three years mentioned before, or, more probably, after the time of his conversion on the highway near Damascus.

"To Jerusalem . . ." The occasion of this visit is detailed in full, Acts xv. He was sent to Jerusalem, from Antioch, to see and consult with the Apostles and Elders about the very question on which the Galatians had subsequently been led astray: see the whole chapter referred to.

2. And I went up by revelation, and communicated unto them that gospel which I preach among the Gentiles, but privately to them which were of reputation, lest by any means I should run, or had run, in vain.

2. "By revelation . . ." *i. e.*, in accordance with an inward and spiritual admonition from God: hence some have concluded that this could not have been the journey referred to in Acts xv., because that was undertaken by human direction. But there is no inconsistency: the external mission and the internal call may coexist: so, in those who are admitted to Holy Orders, they are at once "inwardly moved by the Holy Ghost," and outwardly "sent" by the "laying on of hands."

"Communicated . . . ." and, after the transaction of the business for which he was sent, he took that opportunity to lay before them the nature, substance, and terms of that Gospel which he had, for fourteen years, been preaching among the Gentiles.

"Privately . . ." Not to the fickle and comparatively ignorant multitude, but to the heads of the Church, as Peter, James, and John.

"Lest by any means," &c. Not that the Apostle needed any confirmation of his views, or felt uncertainty respecting them; but he did this in consequence of the calumnious reports which he knew to be in circulation respecting him, lest, if they were not authoritatively rebuked, the consequence might be that his labors would be, by human prejudice, brought to naught. So careful should they be, who are intrusted with the mysteries of God, to see that no misunderstanding be permitted to remain, and to remove all such impediments to the progress of the Faith as grow from mistakes or misconceptions.

3. But neither Titus, who was with me, being a Greek, was compelled to be circumcised:

3. The Apostle now proceeds to the proof that in respect both to doctrine and to practice, he was fully sustained in his great principle, that it is not necessary any longer to observe the Mosaic Law. The first part of the proof is this: that Titus, whom he took with him, and who was an uncircumcised man, was not required, by the Apostles, to undergo that rite, thus remaining as an example of the fact, that circumcision is not necessary under the Gospel.

4. And that because of false brethren unawares brought in, who came in privily to spy out our liberty which we have in Christ Jesus, that they might bring us into bondage:

5. To whom we gave place by subjection, no, not for an hour; that the truth of the gospel might continue with you.

4. The construction of this verse is so elliptical, that the simplest way of conveying its sense is by a paraphrase:—"Titus was not compelled to be circumcised; notwithstanding the fact, that there were then at Jerusalem numbers of persons who insisted that it ought to be done; false brethren, Jews in reality, though nominally Christians, who had crept into the Church for mischievous purposes, the faithful not being aware of their true character, and who, if they could have had their own way, would have taken away our Christian liberty, and reduced us to the old legal servitude: such persons, I say, were there on the occasion of our visit, and insisted that Titus should be circumcised; but we resisted them strenuously; and the result was, that their position was virtually condemned by the Apostolic decision, Titus being received as he was, and held to be in full communion with the Church, notwithstanding his non-observance of the Mosaic rites and customs."

6. But of these who seemed to be somewhat, (whatsoever they were, it maketh no matter to me: God accepteth no man's person:) for they who seemed *to be somewhat* in conference added nothing to me:

6. "These who seemed to be somewhat..." Our English translation conveys, though not necessarily, a kind of contemptuousness or slighting; but nothing of the sort would seem to have been intended. The idea is, "they who evidently were chief in position," viz., Saint Peter, Saint James, and Saint John.

" Whatsoever they were..." A reference to their past history; "whatsoever they were, how humble in rank soever before they became Apostles." S. Paul, though himself of high descent, of finished education, of eminent social position, could not look down upon a brother, however lowly his origin. For Peter, James, and John were but illiterate fishermen; still, that mattered not to him, now that the Lord had called them.

" Added nothing to me." Found nothing in my doctrine that needed alteration or enlargement.

" In conference." When we had fully discussed the subject.

7. But contrariwise, when they saw that the gospel of the uncircumcision was committed unto me, as *the gospel* of the circumcision *was* unto Peter;

8. (For he that wrought effectually in Peter to the apostleship of the circumcision, the same was mighty in me toward the Gentiles:)

9. And when James, Cephas, and John, who seemed to be pillars, perceived the grace that was given unto me, they gave to me and Barnabas the right hands of fellowship; that we *should go* unto the heathen, and they unto the circumcision.

10. Only *they would* that we should remember the poor; the same which I also was forward to do.

7. The work of preaching the Gospel to the Gentiles was assigned to S. Paul; as that of making it known to the Jews fell especially to S. Peter.

9. " Who seemed to be" ... And, of course, it implies that they were, in truth, what they seemed to be; with which, compare the similar expression in verse 6.

" The right hands of fellowship" ... Recognizing them, and acknowledging them by that sign, as being fully Apostles and duly commissioned.

10. This was the holy Apostle's favorite and especial charge; and from this circumstance we argue somewhat of his compassion, his sympathy with human needs, his tenderness and kindness of heart.

Thus far, the conclusion follows, from all that has been said, that the teachings of S. Paul were truly apostolic, and in full conformity with those of the other Apostles; and that they had been approved as such by the Council or Conference at Jerusalem: since neither was Titus compelled to observe the customs of the Mosaic Law; nor did they change or add to the doctrine taught by Paul, while they received him fully into the Apostolic fellowship.

The Apostle proceeds to show, by reference to circumstances which occurred at Antioch, the consistency of his course; and that he had firmly resisted all attempts at a reimposing of the Mosaic Ritual upon the consciences of men. If there had been wavering, or doubtful conduct, it had not been on *his* part.

11. But when Peter was come to Antioch, I withstood him to the face, because he was to be blamed. Understand, that subsequently to the holding of the Conference at Jerusalem, S. Paul had returned to Antioch. Thither, some time afterwards, S. Peter came. The facts, as stated here, are as follows: Peter, on his arrival, mingled freely with the Gentile converts, laying aside all Jewish practices, as well in respect to meats as otherwise. But afterwards, certain Jewish converts came to Antioch from Jerusalem. On their appearance, S. Peter changed his conduct completely; mingled no longer with the Gentiles as he had done; resumed the practice of Jewish observances; and scrupulously avoided any thing which might shock the prejudices of these new-comers. His conduct and example were at once followed by the other Jewish Christians at Antioch; even Barnabas was affected by it: the affair had assumed a serious aspect, and was threatening dissension and possible schism; when Paul interfered,

12. For before that certain came from James, he did eat with the Gentiles: but when they were come, he withdrew and separated himself, fearing them which were of the circumcision. and boldly rebuked Peter, before them all, for the inconsistent course which he had pursued.

13. And the other Jews dissembled likewise with him; insomuch that Barnabas also was carried away with their dissimulation. 11. "To be blamed." To be held as reprehensible.

12. "From James." From Jerusalem, where S. James was bishop in those days.

"Eat with the Gentiles." He partook with them of all meats whatsoever, asking no question for conscience' sake (see 1 Cor. x. 25, 27).

Observe, on this action of S. Peter, that it was an error in judgment and in conduct, but not an error in faith: and also note his meekness and profound humility in patiently enduring the censure which he had merited, for we read nothing of his defending himself or making reply.

14. But when I saw that they walked not uprightly according to the truth of the gospel, 14. "Not uprightly." The path of duty and right is a straight one, while that of compromise is tortuous: he who is minded so to walk as to please

God, holds ever onward in a right line; while he who would satisfy men, must incline first to the one side, and anon to the other; he staggers and wavers. So was it, in that thing, with the chief of the Apostles; now, throwing aside all those entanglements of worldly service, and signifying his right to the glorious liberty of the children of God; by and by, giving hand and foot to the fetters of the old bondage, lest some captious brethren might take offence. He "walked not uprightly;" and the rest "dissembled with him." May this example teach us profound humility, and certify us that we can, of ourselves, do nothing.

I said unto Peter before *them* all, If thou, being a Jew, livest after the manner of Gentiles, and not as do the Jews, why compellest thou the Gentiles to live as do the Jews?

"If thou," &c. Paraphrased, the idea is this: "By your course, when you first arrived, you showed your conviction that the Law is no longer of obligation; for you, a Jew, assumed the manner of the Gentile life. Why, then, do you now contradict what, by your example, you but yesterday asserted? and why would you, in substance, enforce upon the Gentile converts, a system of whose emptiness and uselessness you must have been, and still must be, convinced?" For the course of S. Peter, on arriving at Antioch, had plainly declared in what estimation he held the rites and customs of the old and obsolete system: while his later practice hinted at a willingness to have them still observed and obeyed.

15. We *who are* Jews by nature, and not sinners of the Gentiles,

16. Knowing that a man is not justified by the works of the law, but by the faith of Jesus Christ, even we have believed in Jesus Christ, that we might be justified by the faith of Christ, and not by the works of the law: for by the works of the law shall no flesh be justified.

15. It has been much discussed, how far the remarks of S. Paul to S. Peter should be regarded as extending: after consideration, it seems most probable that they should be supposed to end with verse 14. He now addresses the Galatians once more. The thought in the two verses is this: That he, and the other converts from Judaism (not proselytes from the idolatrous religions of the world), that even they had become satisfied that Justification, viz., a true, spiritual, and inner righteousness, grateful to God, and effectual toward eternal life, could not be ob-

tained by compliance with the forms of the Mosaic Ritual, but must be sought through faith in the Lord Jesus Christ; that they had, therefore, so believed in Him, and, leaving that life in which they had been born and trained, had sought refuge in Him and in His Church; so as to have thereby attained to the Justification which they sought.

"Justified." Justification comprehends two things: 1st, the outer blessing of pardon and forgiveness; 2dly, the inward gift of righteousness in germ, and of a spiritual power, by which a man is able to please God, and to " do unto Him true and laudable service." This is " not by the works of the Law." The Apostle is speaking of the Mosaic Dispensation, which was powerless towards such a Justification. It is only " by the faith of Jesus Christ"—by belief in Him; and it is granted on that condition. To believe in Him, includes obedience to Him. All the just and righteous under the Old Dispensation, are so inasmuch as they have believed in God, so far as He and His designs were known unto them. To desire justification is to desire pardon, true holiness, the power to serve and please God, the peace which this world cannot give. Its fruits are " all holy desires, all good counsels, and all just works." It cannot be bought by man; for it is the free gift of the Almighty.

Justification, considered theologically, is a comprehensive term including the whole benefit procured for sinful and fallen man by the Incarnation, the Passion, and the Resurrection of our Lord Jesus Christ.

It includes the acceptance of the sinner and his pardon; the gift unto him of the germ of a new and restored nature; the gradual development of the spiritual principle, triumphing over the carnal; the redemption of the mortal body from the grave; and the final glorifying of the saved with Christ in Heaven.

Justification, being so grand in scope, and including so much, cannot, as heretical sects have pretended, be regarded at a single glance, or reduced to a single word, either in definition or in explanation: it can only be comprehended by reference to its several causes, agents, and conditions, of which we count the following

1. THE FINAL CAUSE;
2. THE MERITORIOUS CAUSE;

3. THE FORMAL CAUSE;
4. THE EFFICIENT AGENT;
5. THE INSTRUMENTAL MEANS;
6. THE SUBJECTIVE CONDITIONS.

1st. The Final Cause is Almighty GOD, who, to the ultimate Glory of His Name, and to the manifestation of His Eternal Love, has devised the mode of Redemption for the Sinner: we are therefore justified by GOD.

2dly. The Meritorious Cause is our Lord Jesus Christ, for whose sake only, and in consideration of whose Merit and Perfect Obedience alone, without any share therein by any creature, this benefit is granted. We are therefore justified by Christ, and by grace, in the sense of unmerited favor.

3dly. The Formal Cause is Righteousness and True Holiness; for that is justification. By this term we mean to express what a thing is, inwardly, intrinsically, and in itself; the soul of aught, as distinguished from its body or its outward manifestation. And, to justify a man, is to account him righteous, and then to make him what he is accounted to be. Thus, then, Justification, which, regarded externally, begins in pardon and free acceptance, is, internally, and formally, and intrinsically, a new life unto spirituality and true holiness.

4thly. The Efficient Agent is the Holy Spirit; for He is the Worker of all acceptable righteousness in Man: and therefore we are justified by the Holy Ghost.

5thly. The Instrumental Means are: of reception, the Sacrament of Holy Baptism; of continuance, the Whole System and Order of the Church; for we are justified by Grace, and, therefore, instrumentally, by all the Means of Grace. Wherefore, rightly understood, it is as true that a man is justified by Baptism, as that he is justified by Christ, by Grace, by the Holy Ghost, or by Faith.

6thly. The Subjective Conditions are: to its first reception, a living faith; i. e., a faith which includes repentance, love, renunciation of sin, and purposed obedience; to its subsequent continuance, faith and all the works of the life in the Spirit. Wherefore, it is true, in one sense, that a man is justified by faith; and in another sense it is also true, that he is justified by works.

If these Causes, Agencies, and Conditions be borne in

mind, and carefully and devoutly discussed, and if the true and proper sovereignty of each in its proper sphere be seen, felt, and applied, all Scripture will be harmonized at once. But if they are confused one with the other, as some have confused the Meritorious Cause and the Subjective Conditions; or if they are set in opposition the one to the other, as some have opposed the Subjective Conditions and the Instrumental Means; or if any one of them be violently detached and thrust from view, as some have refused to hear of the Formal Cause;—then must the heavy controversies of the last three hundred years be still continued, to the distress of the faithful and to the derision of the ungodly; then can no clearness of mind on these sacred and consoling themes be hoped for; then will the pedantry of private speculation still attempt to thrust into an ignominious background of obscurity the reverend and beloved form of Catholic Theology, saying, We will not have thee to guide and to teach us; and still must ordinary minds be embarrassed by those doubts for which Luther himself found no solution save in denying the authenticity of a portion of the Written Word of God.

17. But if, while we seek to be justified by Christ, we ourselves also are found sinners, is therefore Christ the minister of sin? God forbid.

17. The argument of the Apostle is as follows: "We have left the Jewish System, and have embraced the Christian Religion; we have done this, in obedience to the Lord Jesus Christ, who has abrogated the Law. If now, after doing thus, we be found not merely to be still without justification, but, in addition, actually sinful in having forsaken the System of the Jewish Religion (which, according to the principles of these new teachers, is still binding on the consciences of men), would it not logically follow, that Christ, at whose command we have done thus, is the Cause of Sin in us, as having actually led us astray?" This *reductio ad absurdum* the Apostle uses to strengthen his main position, that the Law of Moses is no longer required to be obeyed or followed by men.

18. For if I build again the things which I destroyed, I make myself a transgressor.

18. The same kind of reasoning is continued; the Apostle says: "I have announced the abrogation of the Ancient Covenant, and the introduction of the New. But suppose that I now

19. For I through

> the law am dead to the law, that I might live unto God.

retrace my steps, and once more enforce the Old? In what an absurd position do I place myself!" In verse 17 and 18, we have therefore two specimens of the *reductio ad absurdum*; if the views of the Judaizers were to be admitted, these consequences would logically follow 1st, that Christ had perverted and deceived His disciples 2dly, that the Apostolic preachers of the Gospel had profanely lifted up their hands to pull down the sacred structures of God's building.

19. The Apostle now proceeds to a thoughtful summing up of his condition under the Gospel. "I through the Law am dead to the Law." I, taught by the Law itself have come to see its transitory hold on me: for the Law has pointed me and led me to Christ, who is its end and object; and having thus brought me to Him, its obligation has ended because its work was finished. Therefore "I am dead to the Law," and have forever passed from that earlier system, "through the Law," through following its leadings and justly learning the Grand Truth which it had to teach. And this has occurred, "that I might live unto God;" that, by Baptism, I might be brought into living communion with the Ascended and Glorified Christ and might receive, in Him, and as ingrafted into Him, the new and spiritual life of righteousness. "I am crucified

> 20. I am crucified with Christ: nevertheless I live; yet not I, but Christ liveth in me: and the life which I now live in the flesh I live by the faith of the Son of God, who loved me, and gave himself for me.

with Christ," to all that I was; dead as well to the old system, with all its formalities and carnal observances, ... to the sin from which, through Christ I am justified. "Nevertheless I live;" I have received a life, in place of that which hath been taken away; the life of the new creature in Christ Jesus the life of him who is made a member of His Body, of His Flesh, and of His Bones. So that it is "not I, but Christ" that "liveth in me;" for I myself almost am lost in Him, and He is of a truth become to me, All in All. "And the life which I now live in the flesh," the life of hope, and trust, and happy spiritual experience which I, although still compassed with infirmities, am now permitted to enjoy, "I live by the faith of the Son of God;" I owe, entirely, to Him, I receive of Him, I enjoy from Him, in whom I have believed, yea, and do believe as the One "who loved me, and gave Himself" in the form of a servant, and on the Cross, and in the grave, and in the place of departed spirits, and everywhere, "for me." Christ, then, is All-in-All to me, and to the whole world.

21. I do not frustrate the grace of God: for if righteousness _come_ by the law, then Christ is dead in vain. How can I creep back to obsolete systems, for justification? How can I so act, as though this marvellous work of Redemption in Him were an old-wife's fable? I cannot thus "frustrate the grace of God!" And if I were to adopt the insane follies of these pretended apostles, and turn back again to the Mosaic Rite for pardon, and righteousness, and salvation, I should be, in substance, announcing that the death of Christ was unnecessary in itself, and fruitless in its results.

With this soliloquy, if it may thus be called, the first section of the Epistle concludes. The writer has now vindicated his Apostolic character as having been sent by God and not by man (i. 1-10); he has shown that his doctrine was not gathered from human lips, as had been insinuated (i. 11-24); he has proved, by historic facts, that it was recognized as pure, full, and sufficient, by the Church assembled in Council, and that the same authority had accounted of the Jewish System as abrogated forever (ii. 1-10); he has declared his freedom and constancy in upholding the truth (ii. 11-14); and he has demonstrated the absurdities which must follow, where his positions and principles were denied (ii. 15-18). He has thus prepared the way for that grave argument which follows, in demonstration of the sufficiency of Christ and the Church to salvation.

(CHAPTER III.)

The plan of this somewhat intricate chapter will, it is thought, be more readily understood, if there be prefixed to the comment on it, an analysis of its contents.

The Apostle, after rebuking the Galatians for the levity with which they had abandoned the truth as it is in Jesus (1), proceeds to demonstrate, by a series of brief, distinct, but connected arguments, that man is not justified by the works of the Law of Moses, but by faith in our Lord Christ.

3

The first argument is drawn from their own experience: they had received the gifts of the Holy Spirit, as well ordinary as extraordinary; and they knew that they had received them upon embracing the Christian Faith and being baptized: how could they then return to an Old System which had given them no such blessing? (2–5.)

The second argument is, that the case of Abraham was a precedent for them: he was justified, before receiving the sign of circumcision, and long before the Mosaic Law was given: the justification of his spiritual children should be like his, through faith, and not through the Law of Moses (6–9).

The third argument is, that all Jews, under the Law, are under a curse; for the Law of Moses demands strict obedience, and threatens vengeance on its transgressors; and since all transgress it in some particulars, and since it gives no grace nor power to observe it, all who are under it are under a curse: from this sentence, however, Christ has redeemed the faithful: to go back to the Law, forsaking Christ, is, therefore, to choose a curse instead of a blessing (10–14).

The fourth argument is, that God made a covenant with Abraham, which covenant was fulfilled in the gift of Christ to all mankind; and that this covenant can neither be set aside nor annulled; so that by Christ, the true seed of Abraham, came benediction. justification. and the inheritance of glory; and not at all through the Law (15–18).

These four arguments having been briefly and forcibly put to their consciences, and to their intelligence, the Apostle next proceeds to answer the objection which would naturally arise, viz., that such a view destroyed the importance and authority of the Law; and he shows what was its true relation to the Gospel; that it was intended to lead men to Christ, and that its scope was necessarily limited, and its duration but for a time;—all which he shows under the simple and beautiful illustration of an instructor leading a child by the hand towards the fountains of knowledge, from which, when the child is come to man's estate, he may draw freely without the master's aid (19–25). So that, since Christ is come, there is no further need of the Old System, but all alike, Jews and Gentiles, are brought, by baptism, and through membership in the Catholic Church, into living union with Him (26–29).

1. O foolish Galatians, who hath bewitched you, that ye should not obey the truth, before whose eyes Jesus Christ hath been evidently set forth, crucified among you?

1. "Foolish." See the remarks on the character of the Gaels; their want of steadiness, their impulsive nature; their headiness and aptness to follow every new opinion.

"Bewitched." There is compassion even in this sharp rebuke; for the Apostle seems to apologize for them, and to lay the blame on those false teachers who had, by incantations and sorcery, as it were, led them astray. The incantations and the sorcery, however, are ever rife in this world; it is a sign of self-will and an ill-regulated temper to be running after men, and, not merely in the last days, but in all time, will they "heap to themselves teachers, having itching ears;" the old ways of the Church are soon forsaken for the devious path of novelty and excitement, and so heretical preachers and "sensation speakers" "make merchandise of" the silly flock of Christ, bewitching them, that they should run after the eloquent lips and the persuasions of carnal satisfaction.

"Before whose eyes," &c. The true preaching of the Gospel is the setting forth Jesus Christ and Him crucified; to set Him before the eye of the soul so that it shall see Him evidently; to make of Him, to the imagination, to the intellect, to the heart, not an historical personage merely, nor yet a dogmatic abstraction, but a vital, personal, and neighboring presence. Hence, too, may be gathered the value of the sacred symbol; the image of the Cross, on our church-spires, above our altars, on the sides of our fonts, in our houses, in the very frames of our doors: this ever-present sign shall aid towards realizing Him, as it were, "crucified amongst us."

2. This only would I learn of you, Received ye the Spirit by the works of the law, or by the hearing of faith?

2. The first argument: to show, that it is not to the Mosaic System that men must look for the way of life, but to the Church of Christ. For the Galatians had received abundant gifts of the Holy Ghost; the ordinary gifts of regeneration and sanctification, &c.; and the extraordinary gifts, as of miracles, helps, healings, tongues, the interpretation of tongues, &c. The Apostle puts it to their consciences to say, whether they owed these to the Old System? whether they had received them as Jews and before believing in

the Lord Jesus? or whether these had been granted upon their conversion and baptism?

3. Are ye so foolish? having begun in the Spirit, are ye now made perfect by the flesh?

3. There is almost a despairing tone in this exclamation: "Is it possible that you can be so foolish—that you can have been so easily misled! Scarcely have you begun to enjoy all this spiritual blessedness, when you forsake the system through which you were made partakers of it, and crawl back to the carnal and vain ordinances of a defunct dispensation, as though to find advancement and perfection from them!" "Post signa, ad circumcisionem devenistis; post apprehensam veritatem, ad typos recidistis; post conspectum solem, lucernam quæritis; post solidum cibum, ad lac recurritis."

4. Have ye suffered so many things in vain? if it be yet in vain.

4. Have ye gone through all the sad, the sweet, the trying, the purifying experiences of your conversion to Christ, in vain?

"If it be yet in vain." A tender qualification of the words just penned, and thoroughly characteristic of S. Paul, in whom appear a marvellous delicacy and consideration for all sorrowful, misled, and sinful creatures.

5. He therefore that ministereth to you the Spirit, and worketh miracles among you, doeth he it by the works of the law, or by the hearing of faith?

5. A repetition of the question in verse 2. "He that ministereth the Spirit," is GOD, by whose power also miracles had been wrought among them.

"Doeth He it," &c. Has He poured out these marvellous gifts on you as Jews, or as Christians? in connexion with your performance of the laws of the Mosaic Covenant; or on you, as believing in His Only-begotten Son?

There must here be understood, on the part of those with whom he argues, an answer, that these spiritual gifts, &c., had been given to them as Christians, and as affording, on their part, the required faith in the Lord Jesus, as the Subjective Condition. This reply being understood as made, the Apostle proceeds to his second argument, drawn from the history of Abraham.

6. Even as Abraham believed God, and it was accounted to him for righteousness.

6. "Even as." There is expressed, in this word, the logical connexion between their case and that of Abraham: he was justified, and accepted

as righteous, on occasion of his faith; and so had it been with them.

"Abraham"... in his uncircumcised condition, and before the giving of the Law.

"Accounted unto him for righteousness." That was the condition required in him, by the Almighty, whereupon He granted him pardon, and the grace of justification, even the gift of righteousness. For, where GOD accounts a sinner righteous, He makes him to be that which He accounts him: in other words, justification and sanctification go together.

7. Know ye therefore that they which are of faith, the same are the children of Abraham.

8. And the scripture, foreseeing that God would justify the heathen through faith, preached before the gospel unto Abraham, saying, In thee shall all nations be blessed.

9. So then they which be of faith are blessed with faithful Abraham.

7. "They which are of faith"... i. e., they who look for acceptance with GOD, to His mercy only, and not to works wrought by themselves apart from Him.

8. In the 8th verse we are taught, that in the promise to Abraham, the conversion of the heathen was had in view; that the promise was not limited to the nation of Israel, but comprehended the Gentiles, and thus, eventually, the whole world. This is, in fact, a point continually insisted on by this Apostle: that GOD's mode of justifying men, from the beginning, has been the same, viz., through faith on their part, and for the merit of Christ foreseen or come; and that the blessings promised to Abraham and his descendants were intended for his spiritual descendants, for all faithful people. Of course, the argument, as against the Judaizing teachers in Galatia, is clear: that Christians cannot need the Mosaic System, as a ground of justification; since even Abraham, the father of Israel after the flesh, was not indebted to that system for his acceptance with GOD, but was justified long before its establishment.

Here let us reflect upon that seeming discrepancy in the statements of Apostles touching the sinner's justification before GOD. For S. Paul declares, that Abraham was justified by faith: while S. James asserts that Abraham was justified by works, and not by faith only. This apparent contradiction may furthermore be elsewhere observed. For while, in another of his Epistles, S. Paul says that God hath saved us, not by works of righteousness which we have done, but according to His mercy; we read, in the Acts of the Apostles, of Cornelius the Centurion, as of a man who gave alms, and fasted, and prayed, and that an angel coming to him from heaven, said, Thy prayers and thine alms are come up for a memorial before God; which things having taken place, the Apostle Peter declares, that God is no respecter of persons, but that in every nation he that feareth Him, and worketh righteousness, is accepted with Him. In the Revelation also, and elsewhere, we are told, that in the Last Day, the final question in each individual case shall be touching the works which have been done in the body. How then shall the seeming discrepancy, of which these are only some illustrations hastily selected, be reconciled?

1st, By accepting both the declarations of the Almighty in simplicity and in an honest heart, and admitting as most true, that men are justified by faith, and also that they are justified by works: if after all that can be said there still remains a difficulty in reconciling these two points of belief, it may be left where we leave those ever mysterious subjects of the Foreknowledge of God, and the Free Will of Man, &c., &c., &c.

But, 2dly, we may be aided toward a solution by bearing this in mind: that the Faith which God accepts cannot be considered apart from the works in which it is manifested; while the works which He accepts are but Faith in action. Faith and works are truly one: the Faith is the Form, and the works are the Accidents: there is no more practical distinction between them than there is between the frame of the living man, and the vital principle by which it consists. To say that a man is justified by faith, is to say that he is justified by a faith which is rendered visible by good works. To say that he is justified by works, is to ascribe his justification to works which spring of faith. Works are Faith in Action; and Faith is works Latent. The affirmative statements on both sides are true. But the negative statements are directed against certain misconceptions or false representations. Thus, when an Apostle says that "a man is not justified by Faith only," he means, that an inactive, unproductive sentiment, as, *e. g.*, an intellectual apprehension or an emotional movement, is not the subjective condition of our acceptance.

When another says that a man is not justified by works, he means that no actions of his can be in any way available, meritoriously, to his pardon and acceptance with God. But whether they speak of Faith or of Works, the holy Apostles are speaking (let us never forget) not of the instrumental cause, nor of any other cause, but of the subjective conditions; of that which God requires in the sinner, ere He accept him. Certainly He does require something : what, then, is it? The Faith which worketh unto obedience. Saint James and Saint Paul speak of one and the same thing: the former of the outward and visible sign, the latter of the inward and invisible principle. Neither of them speaks of an active cause. Faith is not an active cause of our justification; nor are works such a cause: for the Active Cause of Justification is none other than the Holy Ghost. The act of believing, which is in itself a work, doth no more buy the forgiveness of God, than any other work which a man may do. When the formula is used of " Justification by Faith only," it may be taken with two references: for, with respect to the meritorious cause of our justification it is but equivalent to saying this, that there is no Meritorious Cause of Salvation except our Lord Jesus Christ ; and, again, with respect to the condition required in us, it is equivalent to this, that God accepts in every one the sincere belief in Him, and effort to please and obey Him, which, without His grace, we have no power to do. And since there are in vogue and constant use these two phrases, viz., "Justification by Faith," and "Justification by Works ;" it is to be observed of them, in the comparison, that both are Catholic Verities, and both express sacred truth ; but that they differ in extent and range; for the latter phrase is narrower than the former ; it expresses merely the subjective condition, those works, viz., which are the fruit of faith; while the former contains both the subjective condition and the limitation of the meritorious cause. The latter is strictly equivalent to saying, that a man, to be saved, must fear God, and keep His commandments. The former gives the larger thought, that this fear and obedience spring from a faith such that it contains in itself the principle of self-renunciation, and thereby secures to God all the merit, the glory, and the praise. In the Epistle of S. James, which turns on duty and ethics, we find the

simple and more practical phrase employed. In the
Epistles of S. Paul, on the other hand, which are pro-
foundly doctrinal, we find the fuller and more scientific
phrase used, such as befits the higher regions of Theology.
In the same way, among the lower and plainer class of
people, the grand necessity is to inculcate Duty to God,
and Duty to one's neighbor: while it is only the more
educated and trained in thought who can profitably
examine into the mystery of the Justification of the Sinner. The low and the high, alike, know what is the whole
duty of man : but the low know it simply as a positive
rule of life, while the high know it by its causes, and in
its scientific and philosophic form. But, at bottom, there
is no difference.

10. For as many as are of the works of the law are under the curse: for it is written, Cursed is every one that continueth not in all things which are written in the book of the law to do them.

10. The Apostle now presents his
third argument, to show that Justification cannot be attained by the Law
of Moses, as its instrumental cause:
doubtless men were justified *under*
that dispensation, but not *by* it ; for to
justify the sinner was not the object
therein had in view.

"As many as are of the works of
the Law." He means, as many as are Jews. As many
as are under the obligation to observe the ordinances and
rites of that system.

" Are under the curse." Are exposed necessarily to the
judgment denounced on every one who transgresses those
ordinances.

"For it is written," &c. See Deut. xxvii. 26. The argument is this : the Law requires the strict observance of all
its precepts, and subjects to a curse all who transgress in
any respect. But all violate it, in some respect or other.
Wherefore, all are exposed to the penalty denounced.
Observe, particularly, that the Apostle has shown, before,
that the Mosaic Law was not the channel through which
they had received the Holy Spirit : now, he declares, that
no one receives by it justification. For it gave no grace
whereby a man might fulfil it; and it disclosed no final
pardon for him who had transgressed it. " As many,"
therefore, " as are of the works of the Law,"—as many as
seek justification from it, must find themselves disap-

pointed, and must remain under a curse instead of in-heriting a blessing.

11. But that no man is justified by the law in the sight of God, *it is* evident: for, The just shall live by faith.

12. And the law is not of faith: but, The man that doeth them shall live in them.

11, 12. The Apostle proves what he has stated, by the testimony of a prophet: See Hab. ii. 4.

"It is evident..." It is manifest, from another place in Holy Scripture, that man is justified, not by the Law of Moses, but by faith; for Habakkuk says, "The just shall live by faith." The LIFE of which he so speaks is not life temporal; that was what the Law of Moses promised (see verse 12); but it is the life spiritual, the life of the soul, the life which consists in righteousness and true holiness. The just shall live by faith; that is, by a spir-itual life of the soul, or by that grace which maketh righteous, whereof faith is the basis within us. The Law does not give faith, nor grace, nor that spiritual life; therefore it is manifest that no one can LIVE, in this higher sense, by the Law. For the promises of the Law have reference (verse 12) to a lower life; to a happy and prosperous life here on earth: its observance preserves from temporal death, which the Law threatens on its transgressors; hence he who doeth those things shall live in them, shall escape temporal death, shall live securely here. But as for the Higher Life, the Law relates not to it; the Law gives not the true life of the soul, which is to be drawn in from Christ, the Fountain of Life, by faith.

13. Christ hath re-deemed us from the curse of the law, being made a curse for us: for it is written, Cursed *is* every one that hang-eth on a tree:

13. This verse is in contrast to verse 10. The Law brings a curse. But Christ takes the curse away.

"Being made a curse for us..." Being treated, for our sakes, as an ac-cursed thing, and so vicariously de-livering us.

"For it is written," &c. See Deut. xxi. 23. Which curse He endured, by hanging for us upon the cross.

14. That the bless-ing of Abraham might come on the Gentiles through Jesus Christ; that we might receive

14. "The blessing of Abraham..." The blessings promised through Abra-ham to his posterity.

"That we," &c. That, through faith, we might all receive the Spirit

15. Brethren, I speak after the manner of men; Though *it be* but a man's covenant, yet *if it be* confirmed, no man disannulleth, or addeth thereto.

the promise of the Spirit through faith.

of sanctification, promised to believers as to the true children of Abraham.

15. Here the Apostle proceeds to a fourth argument, as to the general scope of which, see the remarks made at the beginning of this chapter.

"Brethren." Note the change in his manner, from reproaches to fraternal salutation, as though he would draw them by kindness.

"I speak," &c. I make use of an illustration, taken from familiar every-day life.

"A covenant..." The idea is a will, or testament; for such an instrument admits to prospective advantages; and so, the blessing promised to Abraham was to come after long delay.

"Though it be," &c. Even such an instrument, if duly and legally drawn up and set forth, cannot be put aside. How much less the solemn promise of Almighty God?

16. Now to Abraham and his seed were the promises made. He saith not, And to seeds, as of many; but as of one, And to thy seed, which is Christ.

16. The application now follows: God made a promise to Abraham. (See Gen. xv., xvii.) He repeated that promise to his seed. But the Apostle remarks, that the word is used in the singular number, not in the plural; it is not, "to thy seeds," but to "thy seed." And, by that use of the singular number, the holy Apostle declares that there was conveyed the promise of the Messiah.

Here may one indeed exclaim, "Thy testimonies are wonderful." For in the mere addition of a letter, in the mere grammatical inflection, is indicated that Mystery which lay eternally in the thought of God. Nothing in Holy Scripture is little or unimportant. Nor dare we say, of any part, of any word thereof, that we fully comprehend all that it means. Oh the wonderful Secrecy and Reservations of the Inspiring Deity, the Holy Ghost! Take one word in the plural, and it shall express a temporal and limited fact, true only of men, strangers and pilgrims here. Yet let that word be written but in the singular form, and there is before the mind a Wonder passing finite thought, a Marvel into which even the angels desire to look. How shall we pardon the shallowness of modern criticism which affects to despise these smallest indications of meaning, because they are so small? Is aught of God's Word small? Is there not significance in every letter, and in each detail? And what were it to us, to have had more of these inspired comments on the phraseology of the Old Testament! Who would have suspected, or have ventured to suggest, that because it saith " seed," and not " seeds," therefore the promise describes and declares the Incarnate Son of God?

17. And this I say, *that* the covenant, that was confirmed before of God in Christ, the law, which was four hundred and thirty years after, cannot disannul, that it should make the promise of none effect.

17. The thought would seem to run thus: Almighty God, long before the time of the Mosaic Law, made a promise to Abraham, to the effect, that through him, and through his descendant, salvation should be brought, as a divine and gracious gift, to all mankind. In that promise lay enfolded the hope of the human race. In process of time, hundreds of years after, there was set up in the world the system of Jewish Religion. But that system could not have been a necessity for men; for, since it was local and limited, if that were the channel of salvation, the greater part of the world must have been cut off. But God's promise to Abraham, to be fulfilled in the Mission of Christ, was a promise to all mankind. No later system, however or for what purpose soever introduced, could disannul that ancient promise. The Mosaic system could not then have been intended to be available to men for their justification: it was but an episode, a parenthesis; the hope, the safety, the life, were in the Great Redeemer the promised SEED, in whom whosoever believeth shall live, out of whom there is no salvation, and having whom, no man hath need of more.

It does not fall within the scope of this Commentary to remark on the difficulties which have been raised respecting the chronology of this verse. To the faithful heart, this is a matter of minor importance; we know in whom we have believed. Such controversies must even be left, to those, on the one side, in whom the god of this world hath blinded their minds that they believe not; and, on the other, to the defenders of the faith, who labor with pious care and study to resolve all doubts that may perplex the mind on such questions, and whose labors have been, and ever shall be, blessed by the God of truth. We proceed, then, to the spiritual exposition of the Apostle.

18. For if the inheritance *be* of the law, *it is* no more of promise: but God gave *it* to Abraham by promise.

18. "The inheritance...." the blessings that were had in view in that first promise to Abraham.

"Be of the Law ..." come to man, as the result of obeying the Mosaic Law; if that system be the ground of our hope of grace and salvation.

"It is no more of promise..." A new arrangement must have been made; the old promise must have been annulled; a radical change must have occurred. But this, argues the Apostle, could not be. For the promise was through Christ, and through none else; and Christ and the Law are not the same, as they who had left the Law to follow and live in Christ could testify; and the promise cannot have been broken.

19. Wherefore then *serveth* the law? It was added because of transgressions, till the seed should come to whom the promise was made; *and it was* ordained by angels in the hand of a mediator.

We come to what is probably the obscurest passage in this epistle; and not merely so, but one of the most obscure places in all of St. Paul's writings. It commences with the inquiry, founded on what has been said, To what purpose then was the Law? or why was it given?

Note, now, what the Apostle says.

It was not the Promise; for it came afterwards; it was added.

It was not intended to be permanent; for it was but for a time, "till the Seed should come."

It was not ordained, personally, by God Himself, but by the ministration of angels; and there was a Mediator too, viz., Moses, to represent the Israelites; so that the idea of friendly proximity and neighborhood, as between God and Abraham, His friend, was lost.

Hence may be seen its low and inferior character; for it was late in time, it was transitory, and it expressed an alienation between God and Man. It was not, in any wise, the Promised Blessing, and could not, by any reflecting person, be mistaken for it.

Why, then, was the Law given? "Because of transgressions." 1st, to keep the Israelites from the sin of Egypt, and to restrain them to the worship of the one true

God, from which they had been led astray. 2dly, to show them what is sin. 3dly, to display, by the sacrificial system, the great guilt of sin. 4thly, to make sin to abound, not causatively, but consecutively (see Rom. v. 20). 5thly, to point and lead mankind, for pardon and justification, out of the Law, and towards Him that should come.

And this was a temporary arrangement, " till the Seed should come," viz., Christ, "to whom the promise was made," when it was said unto Abraham, "in thy Seed shall all nations of the earth be blessed."

20. Now a mediator is not *a mediator* of one, but God is one.

20. This is a verse, the true meaning of which, one may be pardoned for despairing ever to know. So many interpretations have been made, that they confuse the mind. Some suppose the indefinite article to be rightly used : others think that it should have been the definite article or the demonstrative pronoun, and that *the* mediator spoken of is Moses. But let one rendering of the verse be suggested, though with great uncertainty on the whole subject. In verse 19 there are two notes of superiority mentioned, in which the Promise appears far exalted above the Law. The promise passed directly between God and Abraham, for the Lord spake unto him as a man speaketh to his friend. But in the Law, 1st, there were angels to represent the Lord, who came not personally ; and 2dly, there was a mediator to represent the people, who could not approach save through him.

Now, " a mediator," argues the Apostle, " is not a mediator of one ;" but his very office argues several parties ; and these parties hostile ; and thus there appears the sign of alienation between them. " But God is one ;" *i. e.* one and the same, unalterable ; and, therefore, from all the discouragements and gloom of that Law which was ordained because of sins, and which, in every part, bespoke the disjunction of God and Man, we must return to the Ancient Promise, which is our hope and the hope of all, and which God, who is One and the Same, yesterday and to-day and forever, stands pledged to make good to the whole world.

21. *Is* the law then against the promises of God? God forbid: for

21. Is there then any inconsistency between the Law and the Promise? None whatever ; and the proof is,

if there had been a law given which could have given life, verily righteousness should have been by the law.

that the Law cannot justify us. There would have been an inconsistency between them, if the Law, when given, had been made the channel of justification, and the fountain of that spiritual life in which we live by faith; for then we should have found it impossible to reconcile the establishment of that life-giving system with the promise of deliverance through a single individual (for this is what the word "thy Seed" implied). But this is not the case. Righteousness is not by the Law: it is by the Promise: and the Law was but a transient arrangement, fitted to do its work here, and intended afterwards to disappear.

22. But the scripture hath concluded all under sin, that the promise by faith of Jesus Christ might be given to them that believe.

22. And this is clear from the fact that the Scriptures, in describing the condition of men of all states and ranks, speak of them as all under the dominion of sin, and without justification or deliverance; thus exhibiting the ancient design of GOD, and confirming the approach of the promised Mediator, Jesus Christ.

23. But before faith came, we were kept under the law, shut up unto the faith which should afterwards be revealed.

23. "Before Faith came..." before the system of salvation through faith of Jesus Christ was made known in the world.

"Kept under the Law..." restrained under the Mosaic system, which thus served a temporary purpose.

"Shut up unto," &c. Reserved, or kept therein, awaiting the coming of Christ, and the commencement of the era of the Gospel.

24. Wherefore the law was our schoolmaster to bring us unto Christ, that we might be justified by faith.

A beautiful figure: the old system was what a pedagogue is to boys; it restrained them of their liberty, corrected them for their faults, guided them to the knowledge of sin, of self, and of GOD; and thus prepared them for embracing the offer of salvation through Christ.

25. But after that faith is come, we are no longer under a schoolmaster.

25. After the introduction of the Gospel, the Jewish system is needed no more.

26. For ye are all

26. For they take the privilege of sonship; they come of age, as it

the children of God by faith in Christ Jesus.

27. For as many of you as have been baptized into Christ have put on Christ.

were; they are no longer under the pedagogue, but at large in the Father's house, the Catholic Church.

In verse 26, the subjective condition of Justification is noted; in verse 27, the instrumental means.

27. "As many of you as," &c. An expression which the Apostle does not limit, and which no one has a right to contract. It is universally true; all, as many as have been baptized, are members of Christ.

28. There is neither Jew nor Greek, there is neither bond nor free, there is neither male nor female: for ye are all one in Christ Jesus.

29. And if ye be Christ's, then are ye Abraham's seed, and heirs according to the promise.

28. He is speaking of the baptized. There is among them no distinction; all, by that Sacrament, are in Christ, and Christ in them; whatever their sex, their state, or their antecedents.

29. "If" is equivalent to since, as in Col. iii. 1; Rom. vi. 5, &c. Since this is so; since ye are thus, by holy baptism, as by an instrument, grafted into Christ; since ye have been justified therein, by His Grace; and since ye have therein received the Gift of that spiritual righteousness which formally constitutes justification; therefore, be ye sure, that this is the very blessing which was promised to Abraham; ye are the faithful seed of the father of the faithful, and ye are already enjoying the heirship and inheritance under that promise of ancient time.

(CHAPTER IV.)

It is a peculiarity of the style of S. Paul, that a word will give occasion to a long train of thought: some passing expression, which we might have overlooked, we presently find to be amplified and expanded into a large and fair domain of wholesome doctrine, the one idea having suddenly shot into full maturity of power, and proved itself the fruitful parent of a noble progeny. Thus, e. g., the fourth chapter of this epistle seems but an enlargement of that expression of his in the previous chapter, where he has likened the people under the Law to children under a schoolmaster. He says of them, that until they came of age, they were in the charge of that pedagogue; imply-

ing, as indeed he subsequently asserts, that the work of
the said schoolmaster terminated, and must terminate,
upon the attainment by the pupils of full age. This is
the figure, which, through the fourth chapter, we find
pursued, enforced, and dwelt upon, in copious illustration.

And note, moreover, that hereinafter, and all through
what remains of the Epistle, it is the gift of the Spirit, even
of the Holy Ghost, which is dwelt upon by the Apostle.
This would seem to be the promised blessing to which the
writer has referred before. For Christ, and the Spirit of
Christ, are practically one. If any man have not the
Spirit of Christ, he is none of His. And by one Spirit are
we all baptized into one Body, viz., into the Mystical Body
of Christ, the Church. The holy Apostle is speaking,
throughout the argumentative part of the Epistle, of the
Justification of the sinner. In ascribing it to faith, he has
spoken of the subjective condition. Now he speaks of
the efficient agent, the Holy Ghost.

And, that we may know these things the better, the old
Catholic Theology comes to our aid; and that Divine and
admirable science teaches us how we should understand
these darker portions of the Word of God, and how we
may connect and harmonize the statements of the written
word. For, we are taught by her, that after God Almighty
had created man, complete and perfect as to mere and
pure humanity, He did superadd and annex certain gifts
and privileges, not naturally and necessarily appertaining
to such a nature as ours. In the possession and enjoyment
of these gifts, man was raised and elevated; and therein
consisted his perfection as made to be in the Image of
God, as destined to immortality, and as qualified for future
residence, with the blessed angels, near the Throne of the
Most High. This was the true sonship of men; and this
consisted in the Presence of the Spirit of God, the worker
of all supernatural powers. But by transgression man
fell into the bondage of the oppressor. He, who had been
the child of God, became the slave of Satan. From this
condition, the Law did not, as by an instrument, deliver
him: nay, "it was added because of transgressions;" and
its object was to show to him the misery of that state of
bondage, and to lead him towards the One who alone had
the power to deliver him. This was the schooling of the

heir; the heir, but not yet the possessor; the one who was to be made a member of Christ, the child of God, the inheritor of the Kingdom of Heaven. Now, when Christ came, whosoever embraced Him and His promises, was made His son; he came into the inheritance; the sonship, the adoption by the Spirit, even the Holy Ghost. And thus, he was delivered from the old school, and the ancient master; he was a minor no more; he was come to age; and all the possession came to him, through the power of the Holy Ghost uniting him to Christ, and, through Christ, to God.

It is to these divine and sacred mysteries that the fourth and fifth chapters especially refer. Let us proceed to our particular comment upon them.

1. Now I say, *That* the heir, as long as he is a child, differeth nothing from a servant, though he be lord of all;

Having previously compared the Mosaic Law to a pedagogue, and the Jewish people to a child, he proceeds more fully to develope that thought.

"Now I say ...." in addition to what I have previously asserted.

"The heir ..." an heir to an estate.

"A child ..." a minor; under age.

"Differeth nothing from a servant:" is, like a servant, restrained of liberty, and limited in privileges; has freedom, neither as regards his personal actions, nor as to the administration of his inheritance. A slave has nothing of his own; so also an infant heir is as though he had nothing, though the whole estate prospectively be his.

2. But is under tutors and governors until the time appointed of the father.

"Governors ..." persons appointed to manage the estate.

"Until," &c. Until the time fixed by the parent, or defined by law.

3. Even so we, when we were children, were in bondage under the elements of the world:

"We ..." We converts from Judaism; in distinction to "ye," verse 6, where the Gentiles are intended.

"When we were children ..." when we were in the state of minors, of infant heirs under the Law of Moses.

"In bondage ..." under close restraint.

"Under the elements of the world:" the Jewish system is meant, which contained the elements of piety, and the mere rudiments of true religion, retained therein as well for the Jews as for the general advantage of mankind.

4

They "were in bondage;" under a servile fear, as it were, under that system.

4. But when the fulness of the time was come, God sent forth his Son, made of a woman, made under the law,

4. "The time. . . ." the day when their minority was past, the time defined by God, when the full blessing should be poured out upon the world.

"God sent forth His Son . . ." The eternal Generation, of course, is not intended; but that time when "He was conceived of the Holy Ghost, Born of the Virgin Mary."

"Made of a Woman . . ." For "the Son, which is the Word of the Father, begotten from everlasting of the Father, the very and eternal God, and of one substance with the Father, took Man's nature in the womb of the blessed virgin, of her substance;"

> " Deum de Deo, Lumen de Lumine,
> Gestant Puellæ viscera."

The First Adam was created, by direct act of Divine Power. The second Adam was not created, but made of the substance of Mary, by the operation of the Holy Ghost.

"Made under the Law." Formed, thus, and of His own free will, subject to the Law of Moses: not so by necessity, since He was the Lord of that Law, as of all else. And yet, although above the Law, He was willing to be circumcised, to be presented in the Temple, to be examined by the Doctors, to keep the Feasts and Rites.

5. To redeem them that were under the law, that we might receive the adoption of sons.

6. And because ye are sons, God hath sent forth the Spirit of his Son into your hearts, crying, Abba, Father.

5. To redeem them from their state of legal minority, and to admit them to the full state of heirs in possession of their own.

6. He has been speaking of the Jews, his countrymen, as the use of the pronoun of the first person plural shows. He now goes on to say, that the privilege of sonship was conferred on the Gentiles also. "We," before; now "ye" also. "Ye are sons," with us: ye, too, have received the adoption.

"Sons of God." Adults, and already attained to majority; although ye had never been, like us, in that state of pupilage under the old system.

"The Spirit of His Son:" compare iii. 26, 27. It is in baptism that we are made, after that new and living way, children of God; and it is the Holy Ghost, who acts as the Efficient Cause in that divine sacrament.

"Abba, Father." The first word of the Lord's Prayer. By sanctifying grace, the Spirit of God is united to the soul of man; and thereupon, with filial love and desire, the soul cries unto God, as to a most dear Father.

The son of the Living God, as having put on Jesus Christ, the consubstantial Son of God, in baptism. The son of the Living God, as having received the Spirit of the Son of God into the heart, in Baptism, in Confirmation, in the devout reception of the Holy Communion. Abba, Father! the voice of the child, the voice of faithful, longing love. As a devout writer exclaims: "Abba, Pater! quando te videbo, quando te fruar, quando te fruens tecum unus ero!"

7. Wherefore thou art no more a servant, but a son; and if a son, then an heir of God through Christ.

7. It is intended by all this to show to the Galatians the folly of reverting to the old puerile condition in which the Jews found themselves under the Mosaic System. They were sons; they were heirs; heirs, adult, and free, and having already entered on the fruition of the inheritance in the gift of the Holy Ghost.

8. Howbeit then, when ye knew not God, ye did service unto them which by nature are no gods.

8. The reference is to the former condition of these Christians of Gentile origin. "Then," in your former state; "when ye knew not God," the true, the only, the Creator of Heaven and Earth, the Eternal Deity; "ye did service" to idols, to stocks and stones, to devils under semblance of divinities. And in all this, ye were excusable; God had mercy on you because ye did it ignorantly. "But now," the case is altered: "ye have known God," by the preaching of His word; ye have embraced the offer of salvation through Christ; nay rather, "ye are known of God," beloved by Him, the conscious recipients of His unfailing mercies. "How turn ye," therefore, at such a time and from such a point of advance, to the first elements of Jewish infancy,

9. But now, after that ye have known God, or rather are known of God, how turn ye again to the weak and beggarly elements, whereunto ye desire again to be in bondage?

"to the weak and beggarly elements," the profitless rites, the unedifying practices, the effete and powerless formalities of a religion, to which, by some wonderful perverseness, "ye desire," ye have set your hearts on being brought in bondage?

"Weak . . ." as having no power to justify.

"Beggarly . . . ." as containing no riches of Divine Grace, and unable to bestow any.

10. Ye observe days, and months, and times, and years.

11. I am afraid of you, lest I have bestowed upon you labor in vain.

10. He marks the extent of their departure: they had, by sudden impulse, entered with characteristic zeal on the more striking observances of the Law, and such as suited best their carnal taste. "Days," as, *e. g.*, the sabbaths; "months," as, *e. g.*, the new moons; "times," as Passover, Pentecost, and the like; "years," as the seventh of remission, and the fiftieth of Jubilee. From all this, we may see how deep and thorough had been the work of perversion undertaken by the Judaizing teachers in Galatia.

12. Brethren, I beseech you, be as I *am;* for I *am* as ye *are:* ye have not injured me at all.

12. "Be, as I am . . ." as free from all these legal fetters as ye see me to be.

"I am as ye are." Doubtless we ought to read, "I was as you are;" I used to be no less jealous of all these things; imitate me in my abandonment of them.

"Ye have not injured me at all." As much as to say: Do not ascribe my words or my conduct to any angry feelings on my part; ye have done me no wrong before this, that I should resent it. On the contrary, "ye know"

13. Ye know how through infirmity of the flesh I preached the gospel unto you at the first.

(verse 13) "how that through infirmity of the flesh," with great difficulties, and at great personal disadvantage, I appeared among you at first as an Apostle. But this did not prejudice my case; on the contrary, ye despised me not, nor rejected, but with enthusiastic delight received the Apostle as indeed a messenger from heaven, or as though it had been the Lord Himself. Here again we see the characteristic impulsiveness of the Galatians, as well as their fickleness. For the reception

14. And my temptation which was in my flesh ye despised not, nor rejected; but re-

ceived me as an angel of God, *even* as Christ Jesus.

15. Where is then the blessedness ye spake of? for I bear you record, that, if *it had been* possible, ye would have plucked out your own eyes, and have given them to me.

16. Am I therefore become your enemy, because I tell you the truth?

17. They zealously affect you, *but* not well; yea, they would exclude you, that ye might affect them.

18. But *it is* good to be zealously affected always in *a* good *thing*, and not only when I am present with you.

which they gave to him was by this time well-nigh forgotten, and all the enthusiasm had been transferred to the heretical teachers; although at first he had been dearer to them than their own eyes.

16. The alienation from him is feelingly referred to by the Apostle.

17. "They ..." the false teachers who had appeared among them.

"Zealously affect you ..." profess an extraordinary care and zeal for your spiritual welfare.

"But not well ..." but it is not a true and salutary interest.

"They would exclude you..." *i. e.*, from the communion of the Apostolic body, and from all the blessings and privileges of the Church.

"That ye might affect them ...." their object being to attach the people to themselves, and draw them off from S. Paul, that they might thereby attain to the benefits proposed by selfishness and personal interest.

18. The verse contains an exhortation to zeal, to earnestness, to wise discretion, and to constancy; all most necessary for such a class of minds and tempers as those whom he was addressing.

19. My little children, of whom I travail in birth again until Christ be formed in you,

20. I desire to be present with you now, and to change my voice; for I stand in doubt of you.

19. "My little children." A very tender and affectionate appeal, rendered appropriate by the relations which had formerly subsisted between himself and these people.

"I travail again ..." The Apostle had once endured the pain and anxiety of spiritual parturition on their account, when he at the first time preached the Gospel to them. Now, in anxiety for their spiritual safety, he was enduring for the second time those pangs.

20. "I desire to be present ..." I wish that it were in my power to be with you: "and to change my voice," to adapt my teachings and my arguments to the actual

condition of your minds, whatever it may be; this, however, I cannot do, "for I stand in doubt of you;" I am not as well informed as I wish that I were concerning the nature or the extent of your errors, and, therefore, what I say may after all fail, in a measure, of its effect.

21. Tell me, ye that desire to be under the law, do ye not hear the law?

22. For it is written, that Abraham had two sons, the one by a bondmaid, the other by a freewoman.

Here follows one of the most characteristic and beautiful passages of the whole epistle. The writer, after having used towards them the language as it were of maternal tenderness and affection, now changes his manner, and addresses their intellects and reasons by an argument, forcible indeed, but entirely removed from the province of all common discussion, and having a purely mystical and symbolical cast. The words of the text shall first be expounded; and afterwards a general illustration and comment on the whole passage will be made.

21. "Tell me . . ." Give ear, lend attention, and respond, ye Galatians.

"Ye that desire," &c. Ye who have this passionate proclivity for recourse to the ancient system of Moses.

"Do ye not," &c. Will you not learn the lesson which that system itself conveys? For it is the Law which shows its own inadequacy and incapability.

22. "For it is written . . ." For you know the Old Testament history about Abraham and his two marriages.

"A bondmaid . . ." Hagar; "a free woman . . ." viz., Sarah.

23. But he who was of the bondwoman was born after the flesh; but he of the freewoman was by promise.

23. "He who was of the bondwoman," Ishmael; "born after the flesh," i. e., in the ordinary course of nature, of a young and vigorous woman. Isaac, on the other hand, contrary to the laws of nature, and out of time, of a superannuated person, who had not the power of maternity; born of her in completion of a divine promise to that effect.

24. Which things are an allegory: for these are the two covenants; the one from the mount Sinai, which gendereth

24. "Which things are an allegory . . ." i. e., these circumstances, besides their character as real historical facts, were designed, in the order of God's Providence, to display, in a

to bondage, which is Agar.

"For these . . ." these two marriages, or these two wives, represent the old and new covenants; the old, made on mount Sinai, which is the System of the Law, and is represented by Hagar.

symbolical way, the purposes which He had in thought towards mankind.

25. For this Agar is mount Sinai in Arabia, and answereth to Jerusalem which now is, and is in bondage with her children.

25. "For this Agar," &c. This person Hagar mystically signifies the Sinaitic Dispensation; that which comprehends the people of Israel under the legal bondage, restrained by ordinances, and kept under the terror of punishment.

26. But Jerusalem which is above is free, which is the mother of us all.

27. For it is written, Rejoice, *thou* barren that bearest not; break forth and cry, thou that travailest not: for the desolate hath many more children than she which hath an husband.

26. This verse begins elliptically; we must understand it thus : " While Sarah corresponds to, or mystically represents, the Church of Christ, the New Covenant, the celestial Jerusalem, the Catholic Parent of unnumbered children ; to which Communion applies the prophecy of Isaiah here quoted."

Thus, having briefly commented on the words, as they lie in our text, it is next in order to give a clear and full exposition of their meaning.

The circumstances of the Marriages of Abraham are well known to all devout readers of the word of GOD. He had two wives ; the one of them Hagar, a maid-servant, youthful, and in the full force of womanhood ; the other Sarah, who at the time of the events here spoken of, was past the hope of offspring. The bond-servant brought him a son. in the natural order of life ; but the child was a child of servitude, like the mother. While the freewoman, the wife properly so called, became, by Divine intervention, a parent, and to her child, the true heir, were the promises of God fulfilled.

These events were all vehicles of heavenly and supernatural truth. The two marriages represented two covenants, made between GOD and the children of men. The two wives represented two Churches. The two children represented two races of human beings. The marriage between Abraham and Hagar represented the Old Legal

Covenant inaugurated on mount Sinai, between God in the majesty of His sovereign dominion, and the people who stood afar off, and trembled at the sound of His voice. Hagar represented the ancient Church of Israel, the Church of legal servitude. Ishmael represented the Hebrew race: they were the lineal descendants of Abraham after the flesh; and in their Ritual System they were held in bondage, 1st, as not being permitted in anywise to mingle with the nations of the world, and 2dly, as knowing of no sufficient expiation and atonement for the sin of which their services attested the heinousness in the sight of God. On the other side of the picture, the marriage between Abraham and Sarah represented the new and later Covenant between God and Men in the Person of Jesus Christ, wherein He appears among them as among brethren and equals, and unites them to Himself in the intimate relationships of free communion. Sarah represents the Catholic Church, in which the soul is set forever free from the old rites and ordinances of that legal bondage, and in which, by the gift of the Holy Spirit and the grace of God, the convert is delivered from wrath, and has the power of a new life unto righteousness. Isaac represents, in like manner, the Christian race, which are born not of blood, nor of the will of the flesh, nor of the will of man, but of God; the many brethren whereof Christ is styled the "first-born;" the children of the new covenant, standing in that glorious liberty of the sons of God. This is the allegorical sense of the narrative; and its applications are plain. For the Apostle would thereby show the Galatians, how much better, how much higher, how much nobler, is the state of the Christian than that of the Jew; and he would thereby expose the folly of preferring the latter state to the former, since that is, in effect, to love servitude rather than freedom, and to choose the place of the bondman rather than that of the son and heir in the house of the Lord. Thereupon follow the three

28. Now we, brethren, as Isaac was, are the children of promise.

29. But as then he that was born after the flesh persecuted him *that was born* after the

conclusions, or applications; the first (verse 28), that the Christians are the true heirs of that earliest promise made to Abraham, and that the Jews are not the inheritors thereof; just as Ishmael was preferred after Isaac. 2dly (verse 29), that these relations

Spirit, even so *it is* now.

30. Nevertheless what saith the scripture? Cast out the bondwoman and her son: for the son of the bondwoman shall not be heir with the son of the freewoman.

had led to hatred and hostility on the part of the Jews towards the Church, from, which hatred and hostility he was personally suffering, who thus defended himself and argued his cause before them. 3dly (verse 30), that the Jews had been rejected, as a corporate body, and their religious system removed, while the true inheritance was in the Catholic and Apostolic Church.

But, before concluding this review of the allegory, let the attention of the reader be called to the mere fact that it is here before us; and let him consider, from this instance, how he should accustom himself to read the Scriptures of God. An Apostle has told us, that, beneath the historic surface meaning there may and do lie deep veins of richest ore, in the mystical sense and intention of the narrative. A case like this is a key to the whole vast treasure-house. Paul hath led the way; let us follow. Let us not hear the vain and commonplace suggestions of dull brains; but rather let us launch forth freely and fearlessly upon that mighty sea. The few explanations which the sacred writers have given us, suggest to us the attempt to make discoveries; if they had continued to allegorize, as thus, what glorious wealth of good might they not have left us! The word of God is a deep place, so deep that none can see to the bottom; but they are not to be blamed who look into it far and long, and tell us what they see, or think they see.

How beautiful is all this! How that which is to the vulgar eye but a commonplace history, gleams forth upon the instructed view, a sign of the marvellous providences of the everlasting God! Who should have thought of Hagar and Ishmael, of Sarah and of Isaac, under these grand aspects? Or who would have suggested such a lesson from their histories, or who would have deduced such sublime truth from their fortunes, had not the Apostle declared, by the inspiration of the Holy Ghost, that it was even so with them? Yet were their lives prophetic. Hagar, like the lone and solitary Sinai, set as a tenant of the wilderness, for storms to roll around its mournful top, for the hand of the Lord to afflict its trembling sides; familiar with Him indeed, but with Him in His terrors

and in His wrath, not in His grace and His mercy. But
Sarah is the Jerusalem which is above; which is free;
which is the fruitful mother of the Faithful. She answereth to Jerusalem; and Jerusalem is the Church, the Bride
of Christ. Here, then, in the ancient Scripture, is the
living type of that holy city, New Jerusalem, seen of the
evangelist-prophet coming down from God out of Heaven,
prepared as a bride adorned for her husband; and here
the Temple Songs do blend with those of the Cathedral.
For in the former, they sang—

" Jerusalem is built as a city that is at unity in itself.
    O pray for the peace of Jerusalem ; they shall prosper
        that love thee."

While we in our day prolong the words in our hymns :—

> " Cœlestis urbs Jerusalem,
>   Beata pacis visio,
>   Quæ celsa de viventibus
>   Saxis ad astra tolleris
>   Sponsæque ritu cingeris
>   Mille angelorum millibus."

Or again:

> " Jerusalem, my happy home,
>   Name ever dear to me !
>   When shall my labors have an end,
>   In joy, and peace, and thee?"

(CHAPTER V.)

This chapter may be regarded as an application of what
has been said in the two preceding ones. The Apostle
having proved that the observance of the Jewish Law is
not necessary, and that the Church occupies a position
incomparably higher and better than the old Synagogue,
now exhorts his hearers to a fulfilment of their duties, to a
realization of their privileges, to a perseverance in their
holy calling. The whole line of thought, to the end of the
Epistle, is simple and clear ; and what is especially characteristic in it all is this: that the gift of the Holy Ghost is
dwelt upon, as that in which the ancient promises have
been fulfilled to believers, and that upon the said gift, as
actually made, are founded the earnest exhortations to
newness of life.

1. Stand fast therefore in the liberty wherewith Christ hath made us free, and be not entangled again with the yoke of bondage.

1. "The liberty:" a liberty from the old Mosaic system; for that was a double servitude; 1st, in respect to the innumerable rites and ordinances which the Jews had to fulfil; and 2dly, because under it there was no true expiation for sin, nor any gift of God's grace for the attainment of that righteousness without which no man may see God.

Remark also that the Liberty of the Christian condition does not consist in freedom to do as we like, but in the power to serve and obey the Lord. Freedom consists in the power to do what is right, and what is for our advantage. It is the Devil who infringes this liberty; and sin is the real tyrant. We can only be free, by serving our true Master, even God. License to follow our own desires, would be bondage seven times more rigorous; the very name and idea of freedom would be lost. So that "the liberty wherewith Christ hath made us free," is, in reality, our condition as members of the Catholic Church; defended within her walls and bulwarks from the attack and onslaught of the foe; strengthened, by her Sacraments, with the grace whereby we fulfil all righteousness; secured, by humble reception of her creeds, from the paths of intellectual error; held, in obedience to her moral precepts, in that straight and narrow way which leadeth unto life. This is the ideal of Christian Liberty: the being protected from falsehood, whether Intellectual or Moral, and the being enabled to know, to love, to follow, to abide in, the Eternal Truth of God.

"The yoke of bondage" is the ancient System of the Jews' Religion.

2. Behold, I Paul say unto you, that if ye be circumcised, Christ shall profit you nothing.

2. The Apostle now states three consequences which would follow on their persisting in the Judaizing error. "Behold, I Paul." This is the voice of authority. See Acts xv. 1. He contradicts directly what those false teachers had asserted.

"If ye be circumcised," &c. As much as to say: If ye insist on receiving circumcision, as a form of obligation, ye cut yourselves off from Christ: for that is to turn away from Him, as though He were not sufficient for you.

3. For I testify again to every man that is circumcised, that he is a debtor to do the whole law.

3. This is the next of those consequences referred to. He is probably answering some who had said, that they did not, in receiving circumcision, bind themselves to the whole system of which it was the initiatory rite. He replies: if you accept a part, you must take all; you will be counted as Jews, and dealt with accordingly. You must fulfil every thing, or you will come under the curse.

4. Christ is become of no effect unto you, whosoever of you are justified by the law; ye are fallen from grace.

4. A third consequence of their apostacy: If they seek justification through the Law, they forego and lose all the fruit of the redemption which was wrought by the Lord Jesus; they throw away the whole benefit of Divine Grace received in their baptisms.

5. For we through the Spirit wait for the hope of righteousness by faith.

5. "For Christians seek for righteousness by the aid of the Holy Spirit, and by all spiritual works of holiness wrought in faith: while the Jews, on the other hand, seek for justification and sanctity, by a fleshly ordinance and by carnal ceremonies. The former look for righteousness and true holiness, and for the end thereof, even everlasting life, in hope of God's mercy, and in faith in the merits and grace of the Redeemer; but the latter desire these same things only as through the legal rites and ceremonies of the Mosaic System." Such is a paraphrase of the thought herein contained.

6. For in Jesus Christ neither circumcision availeth any thing, nor uncircumcision; but faith which worketh by love.

6. "Circumcision," the Jewish condition: "uncircumcision," the Gentile state. The thought is this: that God, who made the ancient promise to Abraham that all nations of the earth should be blessed through his seed, does not consider the question of any man's carnal descent, but receives and justifies Jew and Gentile alike, on the sole condition of that "Faith which worketh by love." It is the Catholicity of Redemption, which is here declared. And note, that the Faith which God accepts, is not a solitary act of the mind, not an idle and barren attitude of the soul, but that it is a living principle which is perfected by charity and acts by charity; that it keeps and fulfils the precepts of God, delights in the Moral Law,

and performs all pious and holy works. As Saint Anselm has expressed it:—"Illa sola fides, quæ charitate flagrat, et bonis operibus insudat, valet in Christo Jesu."

I have heard this verse parodied by certain sectarians, to the undervaluing of the Sacrament of Regeneration; they have said, profanely paraphrasing it; "In Christ Jesus, neither baptism availeth any thing, nor the want of baptism, but faith," &c. It is difficult to decide which is the more remarkable in such an application, its absurdity or its impiety. For the Apostle is speaking of a carnal rite, while the Sacraments of the Catholic Church are spiritual ordinances: he speaks of a fleshly descent from Abraham; with which there is no analogy whatever in the rites of the Church of our Lord. And again, the Lord Himself did institute and ordain that holy Sacrament of Baptism to be the instrument of regeneration, and to be generally necessary to salvation. (See notes on this subject in my Commentary on Romans vi. 3, 4.) When, therefore, men dare to affirm of that ordinance which he established, and of which such very excellent things are spoken both by the Lord and His Apostles, by the Fathers and Doctors of the Church, and by the Formularies and Sacramental Offices of all time, that it is "nothing," and that the reception thereof or the non-reception thereof is a matter of mere indifference, we wonder and are amazed at their impiety; and when we hear them profess themselves, after all this, the followers and disciples of the Lord Jesus Christ, we are moved to put to them the question which he asked of the ancients, "Why call ye me, Lord, Lord, and do not the things which I say?"

7. Ye did run well; who did hinder you that ye should not obey the truth?

7. "Ye did run well:" ye were formerly earnest, and faithful in your calling. Who hath thus, to so terrible and alarming an extent, misled you?

8. This persuasion *cometh* not of him that calleth you.

8. "This persuasion:" this infatuated passion of yours for Judaism, is not of God, but of man.

9. A little leaven leaveneth the whole lump.

9. "Leaven." He speaks of the false teachers who had poisoned their minds, the baleful influence circulating like leaven through the mass.

10. I have confidence in you through the Lord,

10. He expresses his confidence that they will yet be recovered; that they

that ye will be none otherwise minded: but he that troubleth you shall bear his judgment, whosoever he be.

will be none otherwise minded than Christian people ought to be; and that the troublers of their peace would at last be brought to disgrace in this world, and to judgment in the world to come.

11. And I, brethren, if I yet preach circumcision, why do I yet suffer persecution? then is the offence of the cross ceased.

11. It would appear from this verse that the Apostle had been accused of inconsistency, as though he had, in some places, preached the necessity of obedience to the Jewish Law. He defends himself, by showing that this could not have been the case, because if he had done so, he would not have incurred the displeasure of the Judaizers. For, to their eyes, the "offence of the cross," the main scandal of the new faith, was, that it demanded the abandonment of the old, and implied and assumed that the old system had passed forever away. But if he had preached the continued obligation of Judaism, this offence would not have remained. That it did remain, and that he was so fiercely opposed and so vigorously persecuted by the Jews and their sympathizers, was proof positive that he had not been indulgent towards their favorite tenet, and that he had not "preached circumcision," i. e. the necessity of continuing to keep the Mosaic Law.

12. I would they were even cut off which trouble you.

12. A strong expression, justified by the outrageous proceedings of his adversaries. Would that all heretics and gainsayers might be cut off forever from the heritage of the Lord! Cut off, that is, not from God's mercy at the last, but from their position and their opportunities of molestation and annoyance amongst us.

13. For, brethren, ye have been called unto liberty; only use not liberty for an occasion to the flesh, but by love serve one another.

"For," does not refer to what has preceded: it rather marks the beginning of another sentence; as though it had been, "However, to return from this digression."

"Liberty..." He means, liberty from the obligations of the Ancient System.

"Ye have been called," &c.... Ye, as Christians, and called of God into the grace of the Gospel, are free from the Law of Moses.

"Only use not," &c. That is to say, let not your freedom degenerate into license, and indulgence of the flesh; but subject yourselves one to another in the true spirit of your calling. Probably, a reference to the scandals which might inadvertently be given. (See Rom. xiv. 13, 15, 21; 1 Cor. viii. 9, 13.)

14. For all the law is fulfilled in one word, *even* in this: Thou shalt love thy neighbor as thyself.

14. Compare S. Matt. xxii. 36–40. The Apostle cannot have intended to omit any part of our Lord's word. When, therefore, he says that *all the law* is fulfilled in the precept of charity to one's neighbor, he either intends to speak of the law so far as our relations one to another are concerned, or else he presumes that it will be understood that such a knowledge of our neighbor as he describes is founded on, and includes, the love of God: all the law is fulfilled in this precept, that a man love his neighbor, spiritually, and for the sake of God, and in order to eternal life. The precepts of charity, as given by Our Blessed Lord, are two, in respect of the material distinction of the object, viz. God and our neighbor: but in respect of the virtue itself, the precepts are but one, for the charity is one and the same whereby we love God, and our neighbor in God. Each of the precepts is therefore included in the other.

15. But if ye bite and devour one another, take heed that ye be not consumed one of another.

15. Doubtless the new preachings had excited quarrelling, wrangling, and contention among the Galatians. These the Apostle would repress; he therefore counsels charity, and now declares the end of controversy, which is mutual destruction.

16. *This* I say then, Walk in the Spirit, and ye shall not fulfil the lust of the flesh.

16. The remedy for contention is set forth: to walk in that Spirit which they had received. See remarks on verse 25, below.

"The lust of the flesh." The desires of the natural man: the evil of the unregenerate and undisciplined spirit. For "the flesh" does not signify the corporal habit and material part alone, but rather is it a term expressive of our humanity in its fallen and ruined state, before its reconstruction and recovery through union with the glorified humanity of the Lord. "The lusts of the flesh," are the common and natural appetites and passions of man, in his state of original sin.

"Ye shall not fulfil." Ye shall, if ye yield up your-selves to the Holy Ghost, no longer follow the old law of the sinful nature.

17. For the flesh lust-eth against the Spirit, and the Spirit against the flesh: and these are contrary the one to the other: so that ye can-not do the things that ye would.

17. "Lusteth..." passionately con-tendeth against the Spirit.

"And the Spirit..." *and*, in the sense of *but*, as expressing an opposition be-tween the old and new principles. The Spirit contendeth as vigorously against the Flesh, as the Flesh against the Spirit; nay, more so, by how much God is stronger than Man.

"These are contrary..." These two principles, the principle of spiritual life and that of spiritual death, are so opposed to each other, that there can be no compro-mise between them. If then ye "walk in the Spirit," yield yourselves to Him, fight with Him against the flesh, the victory is sure.

"Ye cannot do the things that ye would." Ye cannot remain the slaves to passion and lust; ye shall have a new principle of life: to sin will become unnatural, through the power of Grace. This expression is parallel to that in the preceding verse, "ye shall not fulfil the lust of the Flesh:" also to 1 John iii. 9. The whole passage may be paraphrased thus:

"The Flesh, that old and fallen nature, full of evil passions and desires, strives against the Holy Ghost, the Sanctifier of all the people of God. But the Holy Ghost, on His part, strives against the evil nature, to reform, to subdue, to change it after a spiritual and heavenly manner. Ye have all received that Holy Ghost in your baptisms, and ye still enjoy His present influence and power. These two, the carnal and spiritual principles, are ever in an-tagonism. Walk, therefore, not in the flesh, but in the Spirit. Do this; be true to Him who hath called you; and the result is sure. You shall no longer fulfil the lust of the Flesh. The Law of the Spirit of life in Christ Jesus shall take the place of the law of sin and death in your members. Ye shall be transformed by grace; until the things which by nature ye once did, delighting therein, ye shall, as it were, be no longer able to do, for repugnance to them; and thus shall ye grow to the measure of the stature of the fulness of Him who knew no sin."

18. But if ye be led of the Spirit, ye are not under the law.

18. A continuation of what has just been said. If they would but yield themselves to the influence of the Holy Spirit, and be led by Him, they would no longer obey the lusts of the flesh, and thus would be delivered from their old condition of legal bondage; being no longer under the law, impotent and weak as to the power of obedience, and exposed to the curse which it denounced.

And another thought may be imagined, as woven in together with all this: that of the difference between the legal obedience and the Christian obedience. For the obedience required of the Jews under the Law, was an obedience of servitude and bondage, under terror, and enforced by fear: while that of the Gospel is the loving obedience of the child towards the parent. We have the spirit of adoption and of sonship; and not the spirit of servitude: we do, for love, what the Law enjoined and enacted under the fear of punishment.

19. Now the works of the flesh are manifest, which are these; Adultery, fornication, uncleanness, lasciviousness,

20. Idolatry, witchcraft, hatred, variance, emulations, wrath, strife, seditions, heresies,

21. Envyings, murders, drunkenness, revellings, and such like: of the which I tell you before, as I have also told you in time past, that they which do such things shall not inherit the kingdom of God.

19. The Apostle enumerates the works of the flesh, as the signs and fruits of that fallen state in which men are servants to sin. The first four appetites enumerated are those of the carnal and material nature: then follow sins of the intellect and mind, as "idolatry," or the worship of false gods; and "heresies," or the choice in religion contrary to the prescription of GOD; together with "hatred," "emulations," "envyings," &c., showing how wide a meaning must be given to the term "Flesh."

"They which do such things," wilfully and habitually, and contrary to the light which they have, are not in a state of salvation.

22. But the fruit of the Spirit is love, joy, peace, longsuffering, gentleness, goodness, faith,

23. Meekness, temperance: against such there is no law.

22. Then follows an enumeration of the "fruit of the Spirit;" the blessed and abundant growth in the soul which is led of the Holy Ghost.

"Against such there is no law." that is to say: they who do these works are under no legal sentence;

5

being led by the Spirit, they are not under the curse of the Law; and if all men were such as they, there would be no need of any legal penalty.

24. And they that are Christ's have crucified the flesh with the affections and lusts.

24. The Apostle in the preceding verses has, as it were, set forth the theory of the Church touching Holy Obedience, as follows: that the Spirit of God is given to us by baptism, in order that we may enjoy that power of pleasing and living unto our Lord; that if we yield ourselves to that divine influence, the habit of holiness shall be formed within us; that a new nature shall take the place of the old, so that to sin shall become unnatural; that we shall avoid and eschew all works of the Flesh, and live in all works of the Spirit; that we shall thus be safe, as children and heirs, secure in the mercy and the love of God. Now, having thus developed the theory, the Apostle, ever practical, regards the actual state of those who are brought within the reach of this sublime system. "They that are Christ's;" really so, truly so; not merely by their outward calling, but inwardly by the glad consent of the heart and will; do manifest this their glorious condition, by voluntary crucifixion of the flesh. This, after all, is the test of sincerity. For it is not the saying unto Him, "Lord, Lord," that can save any man, but it is the doing His will. To be brought under this great system of Grace, is but a deeper condemnation at the last, except a man yield himself thereto.

And here let it be remarked, how totally the Antinomian error is cut up and cast out by this description. For though the motive of the Christian life be love, yet is the manner of it a merciless severity towards that sin which is in our members. For what was crucifixion but the sharpest of all punishments, and the most unsparing of all humiliations? But they that are Christ's have crucified the Flesh. What does this imply? And how inconsistent is it with the views which sink the whole system of the Life in Christ and God, to some mere forensic transaction between the Soul and its Creator and Redeemer! Nay, how can this expression be received apart from the solutions offered by the Church in her system of penitence, bodily discipline, and rigorous exercise of the whole nature? "A man is not justified by the Law, but by the faith of Christ." Is this a light and pleasant doctrine? is, then, justification given without pain and discomfort on our part? So freely given as to be given easily—so fully as to be lavishly? fully and freely, doubtless, yet conferring fully what man does not take freely. He proceeds: "I am crucified with Christ: nevertheless, I live; yet not I, but Christ liveth in me." O easy and indulgent doctrine! to have the bloody Cross reared within us, and our heart transfixed, and our arms stretched out upon it, and the sin of our nature slaughtered and cast out!

25. If we live in the Spirit, let us also walk in the Spirit. 25. This is the practical application and precept from all that went before. And how unlike the language of modern systems! and how fully in harmony with, and characteristic of, the Church's teaching and the Church's way! "If we LIVE in the Spirit, let us also WALK in the Spirit." To live in GOD, is one thing; to walk in GOD, another. They who live in grace, must see that they walk in grace: otherwise, they live in grace in vain. Life is a state: walking is an act. Life in the Spirit is the common condition of all, without exception, who have been baptized. But walking in the Spirit is the conscious and voluntary work of co-operation with Divine Grace. All the baptized do not follow their vocation; it is because all who are alive in the Spirit are not walking in the Spirit. The whole theory of the Church is that of Responsibility for Grace Given: for grace given, by the sacramental instruments of conveyance and reception, for grace which men must improve. And so the exhortations to piety and devotion of life, which we find in the word of GOD, are all traceable to the assumed FACT, that the Divine Gift has already been imparted to the soul. This is the doctrine of Grace which effectually destroys the idea of Creature Merit, and reserves all the glory and praise to GOD.

After the Apostle has thus, by beautiful gradations, come down from the height of theological dogma to the practical field of application in common life, he adds some exhortations, doubtless with reference to the circumstances of those whom he addressed. The break of the chapter we may disregard. His first dissuasive is from vain-glory (verse 26), from idle provocation, and envy and uncharitableness. He had, in verses 13

26. Let us not be desirous of vain glory, provoking one another, envying one another.

and 14 of the preceding chapter, stated, in a general way, the broad precept of charity, and these are applications of that common rule.

1. BRETHREN, if a man be overtaken in a fault, ye which are spiritual, restore such an one in the spirit of meekness; considering thyself, lest thou also be tempted.

So (chap. vi. 1), he dissuades from severity of judgment, probably with reference to those who, misled by the heretical teachers, had lapsed and fallen away. The man overtaken by a fault, is doubtless the apostate among the Galatians; let such a one be reclaimed and recovered, if possible, by mercy and pity.

2. Bear ye one another's burdens, and so fulfil the law of Christ.

2. Reference is still no doubt to the inroads of heresy among them. The load is not to be made heavier by rigor and severity, but to be lightened, if possible. The exhortation is, to show compassion on the lapsers; and so correct them as to support them and raise them from their melancholy fall.

3. For if a man think himself to be something, when he is nothing, he deceiveth himself.

3. He dissuades "the spiritual" from an over-estimate of themselves.

4. But let every man prove his own work, and then shall he have rejoicing in himself alone, and not in another.

4. Let every one examine and with care consider the way and order of his own life. If this review be such as to encourage him, in the testimony of a good conscience, then may he rejoice; yet only in himself, and in the mercy and grace of GOD, but in no wise as contrasting himself with any other to that other's disparagement.

5. For every man shall bear his own burden.

5. The Apostle looks forward to the Last Day. Then, every man shall bear the burden of his own transgression, and then shall it be true that "the righteous shall scarcely be saved." This thought must check all vain glorying in self, and all Pharisaic comparison of one's self with others.

6. Let him that is taught in the word communicate unto him that teacheth in all good things.
7. Be not deceived; God is not mocked: for whatsoever a man sow-

6. An exhortation to the catechumens and to the people at large to remember and provide for those who minister unto them. Which exhortation is enforced by divers considerations of the duty, and the reward, always with reference to the awards of

eth, that shall he also reap.

8. For he that soweth to his flesh shall of the flesh reap corruption; but he that soweth to the Spirit shall of the Spirit reap life everlasting.

9. And let us not be weary in well-doing: for in due season we shall reap, if we faint not.

10. As we have therefore opportunity, let us do good unto all *men*, especially unto them who are of the household of faith.

11. Ye see how large a letter I have written unto you with mine own hand.

the last great day. "The Household of Faith" is, of course, the Church of GOD.

11. The circumstance to which he directs their attention as remarkable, is probably, the fact, that he, who usually wrote by an amanuensis, had, on this occasion, written the whole Epistle himself. It is not "long," as compared with others—*e. g.*, those to the Romans, Corinthians, Hebrews. But it is "long," as a piece of manual execution for one unwont to use the pen, and accustomed to give the work of transcription to another. This fact denotes of course an unusual interest in them; and the thought of that deep interest and anxiety gives us a clear and logical connexion with what follows. For it is as though the Apostle had said: I have been at this pains, because I know too well the insidious arts of those who would corrupt and lead you astray, and I therefore have desired to give you as strong a proof as I could of my care for you, and fears for you.

12. As many as desire to make a fair show in the flesh, they constrain you to be circumcised; only lest they should suffer persecution for the cross of Christ.

"As many;" refers to the Judaizing teachers.

"Desire to make a fair show in the flesh ...." an expression merely equivalent to that of "glorying in the flesh;" see the contrast in verse 14.

"Constrain you," &c. Urge you to adopt the Mosaic Rite.

"Only," &c. Not from any real conviction of its necessity, but from personal and selfish motives; lest they should suffer at the hands of the Jews, who persecuted furiously all who would set aside the Law of Moses.

13. For neither they themselves who are circumcised keep the law; but desire to have you circumcised, that they may glory in your flesh.

13. "For neither they," &c. Those teachers, who had adopted or retained Judaism themselves, and wished to impose it on the Galatians. They did not propose to keep the whole system; but merely wished to persuade

these Galatians to adopt Judaism, in order that they might gain a temporal advantage, and stand fair in Jewish eyes, by loudly insisting on, and taking vast credit to themselves for having procured the conversion of these Galatians to the observance of the Mosaic System.

14. But God forbid that I should glory, save in the cross of our Lord Jesus Christ, by whom the world is crucified unto me, and I unto the world.

14. O noble passage! divine expression of the mind of the Church of God! True, and only, object of glorying, the Cross of Jesus Christ! The Cross, Very and Holy, on which He died! Whose image shines upon the Houses of the Lord, and is marked in the water of baptism, on all faithful brows, and forms the final grace and beauty of the crowns of the kings of the earth, and blazes on the standards of ancient nations! Sole hope of man, and sole ground of our confidence and trust! The sign, also, of the way of life and salvation : for it is by voluntary crucifixion unto the world, that the Sinner lives. To sin, to the world, and to himself, he must die, that he may live unto GOD. Therefore the praise of the Holy Cross is perpetually full, and new, in the courts of the Lord, even in the midst of thee, O Jerusalem. This verse has formed the key-note to many a spirit-stirring strain. Thus, e. g., the following, from the old Hymnals:—

"Crux fidelis! inter omnes Arbor una nobilis! Nulla talem silva profert, Fronde, flore, germine : Dulce lignum, dulce ferrum, Dulce pondus sustinens.	Faithful Cross, above all other One and only noble Tree ! None in foliage, none in blossom, None in fruit, thy peers may be. Sweetest wood, and sweetest iron ! Sweetest weight is hung on thee !
"Flecte ramos, arbor alta, Tensa laxa viscera, Et rigor lentescat ille Quem dedit nativitas, Et superni membra Regis Miti tendas stipite."	Bend thy boughs, O Tree of glory ! Thy relaxing sinews bend, For awhile the ancient rigor That thy birth bestowed, suspend, And the King of heavenly beauty On thy bosom gently tend !
"Arbor decora et fulgida Ornata Regis purpurâ, Electa digno stipite, Tam sancta membra tangere !	O Tree of Beauty. Tree of Light ! O Tree with royal purple dight ! Elect on whose triumphal breast Those Holy Limbs should find their rest :

"Beata cujus brachiis
Sæcli pependit pretium;
Statera facta est corporis,
Prædamque tulit Tartari."

On whose dear arms, so widely
flung,
The weight of this world's Ran-
som hung;
The price of human kind to pay
And spoil the spoiler of his prey.

15. For in Christ Jesus neither circumcision availeth any thing, nor uncircumcision, but a new creature.

16. And as many as walk according to this rule, peace *be* on them, and mercy, and upon the Israel of God.

15. Compare with this verse, the 6th verse of the preceding chapter; and observe that "faith which worketh by love," and "a new creature," are, as it were, synonymous terms. The same truth in fact underlies both verses, both statements. To have a living faith is to be a new creature; and to be a new creature is to have a living faith. Again: God's justification of us consists in the making us new creatures in Christ; while to say that we are justified by faith, is to express that we are saved by being new-born into Christ's Mystical Body. All this interchange of expressions in the sacred writers,—as when we are said to be justified by faith, by works, by grace, by Christ, by the Holy Spirit, by baptism; or when it is affirmed that God requires only faith, or that He requires only the new creature, or that He requires holy obedience,—all this interchange and variety of expression bespeak the entire absence from the ancient apostolic mind of the later controversies which have distressed and distracted the Church. "Faith," when it is spoken of in relation to our justification, includes all works, all rites, all sacramental means: and these last, when they are enforced as of necessity, presuppose in us a living faith.

"A new creature." The soul as renewed by grace, in regeneration and in progressive sanctification: the nature, externally regenerate by baptism, inwardly renewed by grace, strong in that new life, walking in the Spirit, and keeping the commandments of the Lord, in love.

This 15th verse may be taken as a summing up of all that the Apostle has intended to say, in the Epistle. His grand object was, to show that the observance of the Mosaic Law is not required in any who have embraced the Gospel; that the ancient Rite is abrogated and set aside forever; and that man must look for salvation to

Christ alone. This, therefore, he reaffirms once again, as the "conclusion of the whole matter." In Christ Jesus (that is to say, in God's eternal plan and purpose of redemption by and in His Only Begotten Son), the external circumstances and accidents of our condition in this world are not regarded: but the design is, that the whole man should become the subject of a spiritual and moral change, whereby from a sinner he is transformed into a saint, and whereby he may become meet for the everlasting glory of the redeemed in heaven. This is the sum of it all. And the Apostle makes this the text of orthodoxy and fidelity. For he says, "as many as walk according to this rule;" as many as admit this sacred truth, as many as so regard the acts and plans and work of Almighty God; as many as live in the deep realization of this, and strive how they may fully co-operate with Him:—"Peace be on them, and mercy." For these hold the truth as it is in Jesus. These observe the apostolic tradition. These, in maintaining and declaring and illustrating this deposite of sacred truth, are indeed as lights in the world. These are the real descendants of Abraham; the real inheritors of the promise: they are the Israel— not after the flesh, but—the true and very "Israel of God." And having thus declared the rule and limits of

17. From henceforth let no man trouble me: for I bear in my body the marks of the Lord Jesus.

18. Brethren, the grace of our Lord Jesus Christ be with your spirit. Amen.

¶ Unto the Galatians written from Rome.

Catholic Communion, he closes with one remark directed against his calumniators and enemies. They must leave, for the future, the Apostle of Christ unmolested. For he bears in his body, the marks of long and cruel suffering for the truth's sake. He has the scars of glory, and the wounds of honorable strife: all incurred for the Lord Jesus, all identifying with Him, all proving devotion to Him. Let no one trouble him with exhortations to the empty ceremonies of the Law: let no one trouble him by glorying in the state of the Jew. The true and only glory is for him who glorieth in the Cross; and the true and only circumcision is that of the scourge, the rod, the chains, the axe, the implements of martyrdom, last exaltation of the faithful.

The Epistle

To the Colossians.

COMMENTARY

ON THE

EPISTLE OF SAINT PAUL TO THE COLOSSIANS.

CoLossÈ was a city of Phrygia, one of the two inland provinces of Asia Minor. It lay northeast of Laodicea in the same province, and at but a short distance from it. Saint Paul, as the ancients, with but a single exception, unite in stating, and as the words of this Epistle evidently show, had never visited the place. He had, however, despatched thither Epaphras, to do the work of an Evangelist, and he had an intimate acquaintance with the condition of the Church founded and built up by that "faithful minister of Christ." To the Laodiceans also the Apostle was personally a stranger; but it appears that he had previously written to them, and that he designed this letter, which was addressed to the Colossians, to be afterwards sent to Laodicea, and to be read by the converts there.

The Epistle to the Colossians, therefore, is without that special personal reference which we observe in several of Saint Paul's writings. It is such a letter as might be addressed, with propriety, to any one of the churches walking in the fear of the Lord and in the comfort of the Holy Ghost. And yet, its character is marked, and there are peculiarities in its structure and in its contents which make it one of the most precious, one of the most edifying, and one of the most finished and complete productions ever indited by man, ever inspired by God.

When Saint Paul wrote this Epistle, he was in Rome; a prisoner and in chains. It was the time when he was first brought before the Emperor. His situation, so painful and so precarious, may have constituted, under Providence, a secondary inspiration; and there may be traced, in the Epistle now under consideration, the influence of those

circumstances by which he was surrounded. To the
Apostle, imprisonment, with forewarning of execution,
revealed, as near at hand, the close of the earthly warfare:
and, from the mind, which foresaw eternity as evidently
about to dawn, the consideration of temporal interests
must have faded away. So, likewise, in the pressing forward of the mortal career towards its destined end, and
in the apparent neighborhood of the great reward, the
thoughts would naturally revert, and cling, to the remem-
brance of God's inestimable gift; to the marvellous way
of deliverance from the bondage of sin; to the supernatural powers in which humanity had been exalted from
the dust and raised to the full hope of immortal glory.
The Apostle, in Cæsar's dungeon, would turn incessantly,
for light and consolation, to the broad horizon beyond
the living tomb; and in the cutting off of his days here
on earth, he would rejoice in the great career which must
begin for him when this preliminary course of trial had
been run. Thus, while bent beneath the weight of temporal power, he would inwardly rejoice in the omnipotence of God; while held in the grasp of Nero, he
would magnify the Lord who was able to deliver him out
of the paw of the lion and out of the paw of the bear;
while himself a victim to earthly sovereignty, he would by
faith look up to that King of kings and Lord of lords,
who sitteth above all thrones, dominions, principalities,
and powers; while suffering the injustice of man, and the
wrath of every storm of this social state, he would rest in
the thought of calm and deep security as a member of the
Catholic Church of Christ, and a citizen of Heaven.

Under the circumstances now described, what should
naturally be the address of an Apostle, to the sheep of
Christ in the midst of this world? Unless he had some
special object in writing to them, it might be expected
that his thoughts would take shape from the realization
of the position of the Church of the Redeemed as inter-
preted by his own. For the Church is in the world.
Our Lord prayed, not that She, His Bride, should be
taken out of the world, but that She should be kept from
the evil. The Church is still in bonds: She is beset on
every side: persecuted, but not forsaken, cast down, but
not destroyed. Even her hymns and alleluias have a
shade of sadness; it is the singing of the Lord's song in a

strange land; the chant by the waters of Babylon. As an ancient hymn hath beautifully expressed the contrast:

> "Alleluia, song of sweetness,
>   Voice of joy, eternal lay;
> Alleluia is the anthem
>   Of the choirs in heavenly day,
> Which the Angels sing, abiding
>   In the House of God alway.

> "Alleluia thou resoundest,
>   Salem, mother ever blest;
> Alleluias without ending
>   Fit yon place of gladsome rest:
> Exiles we, by Babel's waters,
>   Sit in bondage and distressed."

And thus, the Apostle, directing his eyes towards the Churches of the Lord, would see in them and in their state that which reminded him of his own position; and in writing to them, he might probably address them as, like himself, in bonds; as secure, however, by the power of God; as partakers of the heavenly gift; as needing only perseverance unto the end; as ready to be exalted and glorified, if constant and faithful to the last. And such appears to be the character of this marvellously beautiful letter. It is addressed to a body of faithful men; to whom, by Epaphras, had been preached the word of God; who had received the good seed into a warm and fertile soil; who had so improved the grace of our Lord, that they abounded in faith and works of love; who had sent Epaphras to Rome, to bear to the imprisoned confessor their salutation and their sympathy. To such he writes. To a church which was a true representation of the Great Catholic Body, in faith, in love, in spirituality, in holiness. To a church which presented the mirror of the Family of Christ. To the church at Colossè, incidentally. But, in effect, to the Church, wheresoever spread in beauty and sanctity upon the earth. He wrote, first to the Colossians. But, secondly, he intended this letter for the Laodiceans. Beyond them it might go; it hath gone. It hath come home to every hearth-stone of the faithful city; its sound is gone out everywhere through the Dwelling of the Holy Ghost.

What we have to consider, then, is: that this Epistle is

wide and general in its scope, and that there is in it scarce aught of local or particular. And its whole sum and substance may be resolved into two comprehensive words; it treats: 1st, of Power, and 2dly, of Responsibility. To illustrate this remark, will be the object of these introductory observations.

The Christian Religion is but a development and application of these truths; that Man is fallen, and that he has no power to raise himself from that condition. His rescue and redemption must be effected for him, and from without. The spiritual change which is to be wrought in him, must be wrought by some outside agent, and that agent, it may be presumed, will use external appliances and means to the desired end. These ideas have been rooted in the Church mind from the beginning; and they stand opposed to the notions of an innate power in Man, and of a natural development towards wisdom and righteousness.

But these ideas are not left to float, vague and loose, through the minds of men. They are made practical in an organized system. It is believed by those who have been trained under that system, that before a sinner is able to take any step in the way of light and life, he must have received a Divine gift, to quicken his powers, and to arouse his will. That gift is conveyed to him from without; and is superadded to aught and all that he was before its reception: while the moment in which it is bestowed is that in which his spiritual history begins. He merits it not; nor is he a co-agent in its acquisition. His part is to receive it, in humble faith; and, having thus received it, to keep it safe, and improve it, and hold it fast in active love. Thus the history of each soul is but a history of responsibility for grace received: and they who are condemned hereafter, shall be condemned for having squandered or lost that holy treasure which was committed to their trust.

Again: it is believed, that as the gift is from without, so it is conveyed by external agencies and instruments. These agencies are the Sacraments and ordinances of the Church. For they are not empty signs or forms, but means whereby God doth work invisibly and after a divine, heavenly, supernatural, and miraculous way within the soul.

If now the evidence be asked, of the fact that a heavenly

gift has indeed been imparted, we hold that as the gift comes from without, and as an external instrumental means has been appointed for its conveyance, the fact that the means has been duly used is the first and prominent evidence that the gift has been received. The Sacraments are therefore believed to be, 1st, the channels of grace, and, 2dly, the evidence and proof, in their use according to Christ's appointment, that the grace has been given. And against this historic, external, and positive evidence, no inner impression, no sensible emotion, no intellectual surmise can be, logically, of any weight at all.

To explain: the Sacrament of Holy Baptism is the appointed means of regeneration, and its effect is to make the recipient a member of Christ, the child of God, and an inheritor of the Kingdom of Heaven. He, therefore, who has been baptized, has, in the historic fact of his having received that Sacrament, the proof that he is regenerate, and the evidence that he has been made a child of God. This proof is sufficient; it is unique; he cannot piously demand any thing more.

But the question may arise, whether such a one has continued to be the child of God, and whether he has or has not fallen from grace? In replying to such a question, internal evidence must be received, and no other can serve the purpose.

For a baptized person to doubt that he has received the grace of sonship and adoption, because of the absence of some or of any inward experiences or sensible results, would be from this point of view illogical and impious. But the absence of internal signs might justly alarm him into a fear lest he had forfeited or lost his privilege.

Again: the Sacrament of the Body and Blood of Christ is the evidence of God's continued favor. He assures us thereby that we are very members incorporate in the Mystical Body of His Son; that the forgiveness of sin is renewed unto us; that we are partakers of His favor and goodness, and heirs through hope of His everlasting kingdom. No subjective impressions should be allowed to weigh against this external evidence. It is not feeling which determines a man's spiritual state; and the feelings cannot constitute proof in the premises.

To sum up: the Promises of God are their own proof, and the Declarations of God constitute their own evidence.

And as Evidence may be divided into External and Internal, it is through External Evidence alone that we become assured of our possession of the Gifts and Grace of God; while it is through internal evidence only that we can decide whether we are improving them as we ought to do. Internal evidence is paramount in its own sphere, which is that of Man's Responsibility; but it is valueless in any question of God's Acts and Power. That a man does not feel conscious of a spiritual change upon the reception of a sacrament, constitutes no proof that it conveyed to him no gift, since his feelings have not their exercise in the sphere of God's miraculous operations. They are legitimate witnesses, in questions touching a man's action; but in those which relate to the Work of God, they are simply nugatory. And since the work of redemption is God's alone, and since the conveyance of the blessing to us is also His alone; since Man has not wrought out his own salvation, and is powerless to bring it within his reach, and secure it by his own efforts; the Evidence that Redemption has been wrought, and that he has been made a partaker thereof, must be an external evidence, against which no supposed internal evidence can, in its absence, justly weigh, and which no such supposed internal evidence can, by its presence, materially corroborate.

The system now under consideration, stands of course in marked opposition to the Pelagianism and semi-Rationalism of the day. The most striking point of contrast, however, is this: that Popular Religionism makes Internal Evidence the sole criterion of a man's spiritual state, to the exclusion of all outward and visible signs and sacramental proofs. He who is in a state of grace will feel that he is; and if he does not feel it, then he is not in a state of grace. And so, the child of God will have sensible assurance that he is such; and the want of such assurance proves that the relationship does not exist. The system is reducible to this proposition: that Subjective Feelings constitute the Proof and Evidence of Spiritual Conditions.

Now although they who hold this principle most firmly, regarding it as of vital importance, may not be tainted with the class of views to which it lineally belongs, yet they cannot fail to perceive, upon a study of the history of the Human Mind, that it is but an article of that Rationalistic Creed against which, since the days of Pelagius, the Church of God has had her heavy battle. The leading principle of the Rationalistic School is this: that Man is sufficient to himself without the aid of God; that by the exercise of his native powers he may arrive at all necessary knowledge in respect of belief and duty; and that his progress is a natural development from within. The Rationalists, having laid down these principles, proceed of course to make Internal Evidence the one and sole test and proof, the Grand Criterion. And hence they argue that the individual mind is able alone to cope with all problems; that what a man thinks to be true is true for him; and that we may hold what creed we like, if it squares with our own views, and if we are sincerely persuaded of its sufficiency. Cognate to these profane assumptions is the idea, though held by truly devout and religious persons, that a subjective feeling or sentiment furnishes a stronger proof of acceptance, than the reception of an attested Sacrament of the Church.

Thus, then, may we state the case, as between the Church System, and that now popular in the world around us. The semi-rationalistic mind of the day affirms as an axiom, that Subjective Feelings are the Evidence and Proof of Spiritual Conditions. Where, therefore, these evidences are found, there, and only there, may the existence of the condition be affirmed; so that,

1st, the evidence of a man's being in a state of grace and salvation, must be sought *within* him, and not *without;*

And, 2dly, it is not until a man is leading a godly, righteous, and sober life, that it may be affirmed of him that he is a member of Christ, and a child of God.

Whereas, the System of the Church in contrast may be thus expressed:

1st, God's external witness to a man's condition, is, independently of any feelings or impressions of his, the proof to him thereof;

2dly, a man is made a member of Christ, and a child of God, in order that he may lead a godly, righteous, and sober life.

On the former theory, there is a constant aiming at a state to be attained: on the latter, there is a continual vigilance to preserve a state already in possession. The tone of the former system is tentative · that of the latter

6

conservative. In the former case, it is agreed that *because* a man is seen to lead a godly and pious life, *therefore* he is a Christian; in the latter the thought is this, that *because* Almighty God has made a man a Christian in baptism, *therefore* that man ought to live godly and piously in this world. The two systems are the exact reversal of each other.

Having thus contrasted them, the question now remains, Which is the System of the inspired Scriptures? We propose to answer that question, by an appeal to this Epistle to the Colossians.

It consists of four chapters. The first two may be reduced to this statement or proposition :—

Ye have been made, by baptism, the Children of God.

The last two chapters may, in like manner, be reduced to this :—

Therefore, ye ought to live henceforth unto Him.

But, in these two propositions, thus collocated, lies entire the Sacramental System of the Church, of which the leading principles are as follows :—

1. The conferring of Grace, by and through the Holy Sacraments;

2. Responsibility for the Grace so received.

And whereas Modern Religionism incessantly cries, "Because ye live righteously, therefore ye are Christians;" and until ye so live, ye are not Christians; and thereupon urges men to live piously and godly in order to become Christians; we find in this Epistle a language diametrically the reverse. For it was evidently written upon the theory, that the state of a man is settled for him by God, through sacramental incorporation into the Church; that his state, so fixed, determines his duties; that he is not to look forward to *becoming* a Christian, seeing that he was *made* a Christian when baptized; that the proof of this is external; and, that his actions must correspond to his character and position. In a word, the organic law in the Church is this, that Privilege and Power, already in possession, determine Duty; and not, that we must work up to the attainment of Privilege and Power.

Much of the present misery of our social state arises from the reversing of these truths; from placing the work of man first in order, or at leas· in thought, and arguing

thence to the apparent presence with him, of the Lord.
Faith dies out from the popular mind; because the won-
der-working power of God is neither expected nor believed
in. Hence the idea of waiting for a change in heart,
before embracing the promise of salvation; the error of
regarding sacraments as but the signs and seals of work
already done, instead of the instruments by which, i. e., in
the application and reception of which, it is to be accomplished; the notion that in subjective conditions, and only
in them, lies the evidence to a man of his real state before
God. The Epistle to the Colossians, rightly understood,
could hardly fail of removing the intellectual cloud which
hinders so many from seeing the glorious mode of the
Divine operation; and, subsequently, under the inspiration
of this high knowledge, a purer morality, a warmer love,
and a more reverent fear, might supplant the feeble productions of the modern dilution in which Truth seems
almost asphyxiated.

The remarks which have been made thus far, will suffice
to give a clew to the interpretation which is about to follow. One observation only shall be added. The Epistle
to the Colossians is remarkable for its perfect symmetry.
It consists of but four chapters. Of these the first two
form the former half, and the second two the latter. The
subject of the first half is, The Privileges of the Christian;
that of the second half, His Duties. The two halves are
perfectly balanced the one against the other: as remark-
ably almost as the two sides of the body, or the right and
left sides of the heart, or the hemispheres of the brain.
The point, at once of union and of division is, the very
first word of the third chapter, IF. This IF does not
express uncertainty; it is equivalent to, *since*. And it so
links and marries the two sides of the letter, that all the
exhortations which we find on the one hand, are founded
on all the assertions on the other. But this will be noted
hereafter, in its bearing on the whole ethical character of
this divine composition.

To proceed, therefore, to the exposition.

PART FIRST.

THE PRIVILEGES OF THE CHRISTIAN

CHAPTERS I. AND II.

PART FIRST.

(CHAPTER I.)

PAUL., an apostle of Jesus Christ by the will of God, and Timotheus *our* brother,

2. To the saints and faithful brethren in Christ which are at Colosse: Grace *be* unto you, and peace, from God our Father and the Lord Jesus Christ.

"By the will of God.' It is His alone to send His ministers; no man can rightly exercise that office, under any fancied call from within; all such calls are but delusions. The call and mission are external, through the successors of the Apostles. We know of but one way of rightly entering upon the exercise of the ministry; through episcopal ordination.

2. "Saints:" sanctified through Holy Baptism; cf. ii. 12.

"Faithful:" the faithful are they who believe the mysteries, which not even the angels knew before they were revealed by the Lord and by His Holy Spirit; and who, believing them, lead a life worthy of their high vocation.

"Saints . . . faithful brethren." Sanctified, through the blood of Christ; believing in God's word through Christ who spake it to us as never man spake; brethren of the Lord Jesus, and of each other in Him. A full and exquisite description of the effect of the Incarnation and Atonement, in their applications to our fallen race.

"Grace and peace." "Grace is the seed of peace; peace is the fruit of grace: each the inheritance of the Sons of God, founded on the Atonement of Christ, or given to us by the Merits of Christ."

3. We give thanks to God and the Father of our Lord Jesus Christ, praying always for you,

4. Since we heard of your faith in Christ Jesus, and of the love

3, 4. From these verses may be formed a just opinion of the noble character of the Church-life throughout that region; not merely at Colosse, but also at Laodicea, for which also the letter was intended.

which ye have to all the saints,

5. For the hope which is laid up for you in heaven, whereof ye heard before in the word of the truth of the gospel;

5. "The hope," *i. e.*, of future glory and blessedness. For heavenly joys are the promised reward of faith and love, and in view of them should men be diligent in every good work.

"Whereof:" of which blessed store of hope and coming joy.

"The word of the truth of the Gospel . . ." The most true and very certain word of the Gospel.

6. Which is come unto you, as *it is* in all the world; and bringeth forth fruit, as *it doth* also in you, since the day ye heard *of it,* and knew the grace of God in truth:

6. "In all the world." Either the Apostle means, in those parts of the world then known and accessible; or else, perhaps, and probably, he speaks under an impulse of prophecy, and looks to the day when the earth shall be full of the knowledge of the Lord, as the waters cover the sea. Already is the sound of the Gospel, potentially, gone out into all lands: for the Kingdom of Satan and of Sin is doomed; and the triumph of the Cross, though deferred, is finally sure. To the ears of fiends, and of the lost spirits, the Gospel is indeed come into all the world.

"As it doth," &c. Another intimation of the faithfulness and worthiness of the Colossians who were in Christ.

"The grace of God in truth." The truth and certainty of the Grace of God; its life-giving power, and the permanency of its effects in the leavening, not merely of the individual being, but also of the whole mass of humanity.

7. As ye also learned of Epaphras our dear fellowservant, who is for you a faithful minister of Christ;

8. Who also declared unto us your love in the Spirit.

7, 8. It has been inferred, from these verses, that Epaphras had preached the Gospel to them; that he was their Apostle, and not S. Paul; that he had been sent to them by S. Paul; and that he had returned to visit Paul at Rome, bearing with him the love and good wishes of the brethren.

"Love in the Spirit:" such love as is manifestly inspired and poured into the heart by the Holy Ghost.

9. For this cause we also, since the day we heard *it,* do not cease to pray for you, and to desire that ye might be

9. How profound the impression which must have been made upon the Apostle's mind! and how deep the relief found by him, amid chains and captivity, in meditating upon the

filled with the knowl- work of grace among these good and
edge of his will in all faithful men!
wisdom and spiritual
understanding;   "Filled with the knowledge of His
                          will:" *i. e.*, with a more full, more
deep, more exact knowledge; with such an enlarged and
increased comprehension of the heavenly mysteries, as
might be deemed meet to be enjoyed by them in respect
of their diligent use of all that they had already received.
For as we rightly use them, God's gifts increase in value
with us.

"In all wisdom and spiritual understanding." By
abundant gifts of the same. Wisdom is concerned about
the reception and following out of mysteries; understanding, about their practical application. And so, in Holy
Confirmation, the sevenfold gifts of the Holy Ghost are
enumerated, as also in the hymn, *Veni Creator Spiritus*,
as follows:—

"The Spirit of Wisdom and Understanding; the Spirit
of Counsel and Ghostly Strength; the Spirit of Knowledge
and true Godliness; and the Spirit of Holy Fear:" each
having its distinct and proper meaning. The Gift of Wisdom being that, whereby we devoutly receive the Mysteries of the Faith: that of Understanding being the gift
whereby we apply the Creed in a practical manner for the
guidance of our lives: as also Counsel, whereby we choose
the good and decline from the evil; Ghostly Strength,
whereby we stand firm in the Lord, resisting the adversary; Knowledge, whereby we test by our high axioms of
Divine truth all the ways, the devices, the imaginings of
men, and all that calls itself science and knowledge, but
for the most part wrongly so; True Godliness, whereby
a man grows more and more into the image and likeness
of God; and Holy Fear, which holds to full consistency
the circle of the life, in dread of the Majesty and Greatness
of Him with whom we have to do.

                          10. "Worthy of the Lord . . . ."
10. That ye might Worthy of the inestimable privileges
walk worthy of the
Lord unto all pleasing, conferred by Him; worthy of that
being fruitful in every great and glorious condition which
good work, and in- the Apostle presently so splendidly
creasing in the knowl- developes and describes.
edge of God;
                          "Unto all pleasing . . ." So as in
all things to please Him.

11. Strengthened with all might, according to his glorious power, unto all patience and longsuffering with joyfulness;

11. "Strengthened," &c. Even as they actually were. The mighty power of the Holy Ghost is referred to.

"His glorious power." We may meditate long on such expressions as this, before we feel what they imply. There is a certain glory, hidden from the common view, but now and then flashing forth clear and dazzling, through all the process and work of our redemption. It was seen in Our Lord, at times; it has been reflected in His Saints; it is ever near and ready to be revealed; it shall blaze in pre-eminent splendors around the pathway of His Second Advent. But though we see it not, yet is His power always attended with the near radiance and glory; and although there be a hiding thereof, yet this is perhaps intended mercifully, since we should not be able to endure its manifestation. When Saul beheld that "glorious power" on the way to Damascus, he and all his company fell to the earth together, and he was for three days without speech or sight. This same glory is near us, even round about every font and above every altar, and through the shrines and sanctuaries of God: but we see it not now, for it is in mercy hidden from our eyes.

"O God of mercy, God of might,
How should pale sinners bear the sight,
If, as Thy power is surely here,
Thine open glory should appear?"

"Patience... Longsuffering." At these words we remember the Apostle in his dungeon; there is a gleam of personality, strong and clear, along the line of the thought. "With joyfulness," also: for he, in his bonds, felt not their power, for the glorious hope of the final deliverance.

12. Giving thanks unto the Father, which hath made us meet to be partakers of the inheritance of the saints in light:

12. Here begins that grand and sublime description of the privileges and position of the faithful, which makes up the greater part of the first two chapters.

"Giving thanks..." The Apostle speaks in his own person.

"Unto the Father." The form of this thanksgiving borders on the Sacramental and the Eucharistic. For in the Holy Eucharist, the oblation is made, not to the Holy Trinity, but to the Father; as it is said by the priest, "by whom and with whom, in the unity of the Holy Ghost, all honor and glory be unto Thee, O Father Almighty, world without end. Amen."

"Made us meet..." fit or worthy. Let modern schools settle it among themselves how they will understand this language. The Church hath ever acknowledged a worthiness of congruity in the Saints. See Rev. iii. 4; S. Luke xxi. 36; 2 Thess. i. 5, 6, &c., &c. Merit of condignity, involving creature claim and a right to the gift of God, is what the Church and the Scriptures deny as possible in any case. But merit of congruity, or fitness and suitableness, has ever been recognized as necessary, and is everywhere expressed or implied throughout the Scriptures The bad and most offensive sense of *merit*, is not its scriptural nor its ancient meaning, but the gross corruption of later and depraved ages.

"Saints in light." The Holy Angels are probably meant; and the idea is to express the opening to man a way into the very inmost shrines and tabernacles in Heaven, where the Angels continually do cry, and where Cherubim and Seraphim respond everlastingly in the praises of the Most Holy. This is the "inheritance" promised to "them that love him."

13. Who hath delivered us from the power of darkness, and hath translated *us* into the kingdom of his dear Son:

13. "The power of darkness..." The kingdom of Satan, and the influences of his incantations.

"The Kingdom of His dear Son..." That is, the Church of Christ, whereof Holy Baptism is the door. For Christ is the Light; and His Church is the Kingdom of Light. At her gates the powers of darkness are exorcised and cast out; and in her the Reason rejoices in the true illumination from God.

"His dear Son..." This term of love and deep affection would seem to be spontaneously rushing to the Apostle's thought, in view of what immediately follows, the pouring out of that most precious Blood. "His dear Son!" Dear, indeed; dear to all hearts; dear, for what He did;

"Jesu, dulcis memoria,
Dans vera cordis gaudia;

Sed super mel et omnia,
Ejus dulcis præsentia.

"Nil canitur suavius,
Nil auditur jucundius,
Nil cogitatur dulcius,
Quam Jesus Dei Filius."

Note also, that it is to Him, the Son of God, that the following sublime verses refer. And it would be impossible to describe Omnipotence and Absolute Deity, more clearly than they are set forth in the ensuing terms. The power of language could go no further; yet all that is predicated, is predicated of Him who shed His Blood for us upon the cross of shame.

14. In whom we have redemption through his blood, *even* the forgiveness of sins:

14. "Redemption through His Blood..." For He is the vicarious sin-offering, the propitiation for all the sins of all the world. In which redemption the first gift is that of pardon.

15. Who is the image of the invisible God, the firstborn of every creature.

15. "The Image," is doubtless intended to stand in contrast with the Invisibility of God. Thus, we get the idea, expressed by the Lord's own lips: "no man hath seen God at any time: the only-begotten Son, which is in the bosom of the Father, He hath revealed Him." The Divine Nature, the Divine Substance, can no mortal possibly behold. But, veiled in Flesh, it is revealed in Christ. His Humanity is the Image, the "Imago," by looking upon which, we form the conception of Almighty God.

The Son of God, co-equal and co-eternal with the Father, and thus, in power, in glory, in all things like unto Him, and thus perpetually His Image and perfect representment, clad afterwards in flesh, becomes visible to men, and thus reveals to them a true and just image of the Father.

"The Firstborn of every creature." Begotten before any thing was created. And so more excellent than any creature. For all creatures were made by Him. He preceded them all in eternity; He made them all in time. "Quas omnes æternitate præcedit, et quas omnes in tempore creavit." Lest any should be misled by a heretical gloss, as though Christ were a creature Himself, let him look on, and be silent, and adore.

16. For by him were all things created, that are in heaven, and that are in earth, visible and invisible, whether *they* **be thrones, or dominions, or principalities, or powers: all things were created by him, and for him:**

If this language does not express Absolute Divinity, no language is capable of expressing it.

"By Him." By Christ.

"All things..." therefore He was not created, otherwise this were not true. Cf. S. John's Gospel, i. 3, 10.

"In Heaven... in earth:" terms of universal comprehension.

"Visible and invisible..." lest any should suppose that spiritual essences were to be excepted.

"Thrones, Dominions, Principalities, Powers..." Not merely the ordinary angels, but those of highest degree; for these terms are the titles of ranks and grades in the angelic hosts. All, alike, were made by Christ, and without Him was not any Angel or Archangel made that was made.

"By Him..." As the Agent.

"For Him..." As the First End of their existence; lest any heretical gloss should creep in as though He were merely an instrument, and as though they were intended, not for His glory and supreme honor, but for some other.

17. And he is before all things, and by him all things consist.

17. "Before all things..." because eternal.

"All... consist." He not merely created all, but sustains, supports, upholds all things.

18. And he is the head of the body, the church: who is the beginning, the firstborn from the dead; that in all *things* **he might have the preeminence.**

18. In the former part of this sublime description, the Lord is spoken of in His divine character. But now, He is spoken of as the Man. For in His humanity He is the head of the Church; and as Man, was He the First Fruits of the Resurrection. A devout writer has admirably contrasted the aims and scope of these verses as follows:

"He who, as GOD, is before all things, and by whom all things consist;

"As Man, is the head of the Church, the fountain of all knowledge and of every motion of supernatural grace, of whose fulness have all we received.

"He who, as GOD, is the beginning of all things;

"As Man, is the beginning, the fount, the author of resurrection to eternal life.

" He who, as God, is the first-begotten of every creature;
"As Man, is the first-begotten of them that rise again to
immortality."

Marvellous, that after all this, any could be found so
blind, so rash as to impugn the true, the full, the perfect
deity of the Lord Christ! Yet there is no length too
great, too distant, whither the unbridled temper of doubtful and presumptuous man may not perchance conduct him.
But which shall we hold to be the right, the reasonable
interpreter of Holy Scripture; the philosophic school,
which withholds the full confession, and would still raise
a doubt whether Christ be really divine; or that Church
which believes "in One Lord Jesus Christ, the only-begotten Son of God, begotten of His Father before all
worlds, God of God, Light of Light, Very God of Very
God, begotten, not made, being of one substance with the
Father; By whom all things were made?" Which of
these two witnesses speaks, of itself? and which hath the
mind of the Spirit?

"That in all things He might have the pre-eminence."
In respect to His Divine Nature and to His Human. As
God, He hath the pre-eminence over all that is not God,
as the One by whom, in whom, and unto whom all things
are and were created. As Man, He hath the pre-eminence
in His Church, which shall finally break to pieces all the
kingdoms of the earth and the glory of them.

"The first-born from the dead....." Not first in
time, but first in causality. Nay, first in time also, if
we think of Him as the one over whom Death hath no
more dominion. And first, since His Resurrection was
the exemplar and cause of all others that ever were or
shall be.

19. For it pleased   19. "In Him," to wit, as Man; for
the Father that in him   in Him as God, all fulness dwelt al-
should all fulness dwell;   ready. But on the exaltation and
glorifying of Christ, the Humanity came to receive in
time all that the Divinity had from Eternity, so far as
Human Nature was capable thereof. By bearing this in
mind many obscure passages in Holy Scripture become
clear. See, for instance, Heb. i. 4, where it is said of Our
Lord that he was made better than the angels. But in
this Epistle we have just read that the angels were created
by Him. How can it be said of the Creator that He was

made to become better than His own works? Many other instances may be given, on which the same difficulty would arise. But the solution lies here: He, who was eternally equal with the Father, became Man, thereby descending to the state of a servant: but thereupon He was exalted, as Man, so as to become, in respect to His Humanity, all that He had been, in respect to His Deity, from eternity.

Among the fathers we find this view clearly and grandly set forth, but nowhere so fully or splendidly as in the writings of Saint Athanasius. The following extracts are given, in illustration of this remark.

" In the beginning was the Word, and the Word was with God, and the Word was God. But, for our sakes, afterwards, the Word was made flesh. And the term in question, 'wherefore also God hath highly exalted Him,' (Phil. ii. 6), does not signify that the substance of the Word was exalted, for He was ever and is equal to God, but the exaltation is of the Manhood... For of this was Man's nature in want, because of the humble estate of the flesh and of death... therefore, as Man, He is said, *because of us*, and *for us*, to be highly exalted, that as by His Death we all died in Christ, so again in the Christ Himself we might be highly exalted, being raised from the dead and ascending into heaven whither the forerunner is for us entered.

" He sanctifies Himself (to wit as Man), not that the Word may become holy, but that He Himself may in Himself sanctify all of us.

" God exalted Him, not that He Himself should be exalted, for He is the Highest; but that He may become righteousness for us, and we may be exalted in Him... and if the Son be righteousness, then He is not exalted as being Himself in need, but it is we who are exalted in that righteousness which is He...

" For the Word, in receiving a Body, deified (ἐθεοποίησεν) that which He put on, nay, gave it graciously to the race of men...

" For whereas the Powers in Heaven, both Angels and Archangels were ever worshipping the Lord, as they are now worshipping Him in the Name of Jesus, this is our grace and high exaltation, that even when He became Man the Son of God is worshipped, and the Heavenly

Powers are not startled at seeing all of us, who are of one body with Him, introduced into their realms...

"Therefore if even before the world was made the Son had that glory and was Lord of Glory, and Highest over all, and descended from Heaven, and is ever to be worshipped, it follows that He had no promotion from His descent, but rather Himself promoted the things which needed promotion... and He descended to effect their promotion."

Thus far the holy father, upon the place in Philippians ii. 9, 10. The following remarks of his, on Psalm xlv. 7, 8, are to the same effect:

"Therefore He is here said to be anointed, not that He may become God, for He was so even before; nor that He may become King, for He had the kingdom eternally, existing as God's Image, as the sacred oracle shows; but in our behalf is this written as before. For the Israelitish kings upon their being anointed then became kings, not being so before; but the Saviour, on the contrary, being God and ever ruling in the Father's Kingdom, and being Himself the Dispenser of the Holy Ghost, nevertheless is here said to be anointed, that, as before, being said as man to be anointed with the Spirit, He might provide for us anew, not only exaltation and resurrection, but the indwelling and intimacy of the Spirit...

"The Spirit's descent on Him in Jordan was a descent on us, because of His bearing our Body. And it did not take place for promotion (ἐπὶ βελτιώσει) to the Word, but again for our sanctification, that we might share His anointing, and of us it might be said, Know ye not that ye are God's temple, and the Spirit of God dwelleth in you? (1 Cor. iii. 16.) For when the Lord, as Man, was washed in Jordan, it was we who were washed in Him and by Him; and when He received the Spirit, it was we who by Him were made recipients thereof...

"If, as the Lord Himself has said, the Spirit is His, and He takes of His and sends it, it is not the Word, considered as the Word and Wisdom, who is anointed with the Spirit which He Himself gives; but the Flesh assumed by Him which is anointed in Him and by Him, that the sanctification coming to the Lord as Man, may come to all men from Him."

Quotations might be multiplied; but these are sufficient

for our purpose. The Athanasian view is this: The Word and Son of God had the fulness of Deity from the beginning. In time, this Divine Person became incarnate. He gained naught thereby, unto Himself, since personally He was incapable of advancement. But the nature which He assumed was advanced, and promoted, and glorified. Beginning to exist, in a new way, as Man, He came to possess, all over again, in that Humanity of His, all that He had before in His Divine Nature, so far as it was possible without absorbing or annihilating or transubstantiating the Manhood. All this was done for us. And all the expressions in the Holy Scriptures, touching Christ's being "exalted," or "receiving," or "being made," or "becoming," are to be understood of the Humanity, and not of the Deity.

Whoever would see more of the old Church mind on these heavenly themes, is referred to S. Athanasius, Discourses against the Arians; S. Leo, Epistles; and S. Gregory Nazianzen, Theological Orations.

20. And, having made peace through the blood of his cross, by him to reconcile all things unto himself; by him, *I say,* whether *they be* things in earth, or things in heaven.

20. "Having made peace." Sin was the cause of hostility between heaven and earth: but Christ, by His death, destroyed the cause of alienation, and thus pacified all things.

"Things in earth and things in heaven," are evidently men and angels. This is said, doubtless, with reference to the angelic chorus on the night of the Nativity, "Peace on earth, good will to men," or "to men of good-will;" hominibus bonæ voluntatis. We cannot comprehend the full extent of these divine statements as to the universal pacification and reconciliation of things above and things below; because we know not the extent of the disorder which Sin has worked through the whole universe. But one thing is clear. The effects of the Lord's Incarnation, Atonement, and Triumphant Exaltation to Glory, are by no means to be limited to this one globe, and to the inhabitants thereof: they are felt, beyond; they are powerful to some grand results, even in the spheres nearest to the Eternal Throne. The Angels are now interested in the Mysteries and Rites of the Militant Church (see 1 Peter i. 12). And it is a part, nay the sum and conclusion, of the Plan of God, to gather into

7

One in Christ, all things, in Heaven and on Earth. So that nothing can be more unsatisfying than the view which would refuse to take in all these sublime relations, and limit itself to the narrow radius of the orbit of the earth. (See remarks on Romans viii. 19–22.)

21. And you, that were sometime alienated and enemies in *your* mind by wicked works, yet now hath he reconciled

21. "And you." Here the thought contracts; in the preceding verse it is wide enough to hold the Universe enclosed.

"Sometime:" before their call and conversion to the Catholic faith.

"Alienated in mind:" as not having the true knowledge of GOD: and so "enemies," for he that is not with Him is against Him.

22. In the body of his flesh through death, to present you holy and unblameable and unreproveable in his sight;

22. "In the body of His Flesh." *i. e*, through assuming our common Humanity.

"Through death:" and by dying for us, offering Himself the true atonement.

"To present you," &c. For this is the end of all our Lord's work; that we may be holy, even as He is holy. "Holy," as sanctified by the Holy Ghost, which is shed upon us abundantly through the washing of regeneration; "unblameable and unreproveable," in respect to the accusations of our adversary, the accuser of the brethren; for "who shall lay any thing to the charge of GOD's elect? It is GOD that justifieth; who is he that condemneth?" &c., &c., &c. See Romans, viii. 33, 34.

23. If ye continue in the faith grounded and settled, and *be* not moved away from the hope of the gospel, which ye have heard, *and* which was preached to every creature which is under heaven; whereof I Paul am made a minister;

23. "To every creature which is under heaven." This may be an instance of hyperbole, as though the Apostle meant, "to many, to very many, as well in the West as in the East, as well in the North and in the far islands of the sea, as in the South and in the pleasant lands; not, however, absolutely to all." But it may be reverently suggested, whether some wider sense may not have been intended by the Spirit; whether the effect of our Lord's work does not extend far beyond our gaze; and whether the creatures which He made, which He sustains, which He loves, should be shut

out, by our criticism, from some participation in His crowning act of mercy, even His Incarnation and Passion? At least, let us interpret thus; that "every creature," means, "every being capable of receiving aid and blessing from the redemption;" and let us leave it to GOD to say, and to tell us, who and what, and where they are that may fall within this category. What a marvellous lighting up of dark places will there be, at the Last Great Day! And how may we then, perchance, be forced to blush when we look back upon the sum and amount of our former knowledge!

24. Who now rejoice in my sufferings for you, and fill up that which is behind of the afflictions of Christ in my flesh for his body's sake, which is the church:

24. "My sufferings ..." for he was in prison.

"For you ..." i. e., for you as members of the Church. Suffering for the benefit of the Church, was suffering for all its members individually.

"And fill up that," &c. To suppose the intention of the Apostle to be, that our Lord's sufferings were anywise incomplete, that He had left any thing undone which He might or ought to have done, or that His work needed to be finished by any mortal;—this would be the height of folly and presumption.

The difficulty, if there be one, in this verse, lies in the words, "of Christ." Some render "of" in the sense of "for," and understand the Apostle, when he speaks of "the afflictions of Christ," to mean "afflictions borne for Christ's sake." But let us rather take it in the sense of, "imposed by Christ," "appointed and ordained by Christ." Then the sense will be as follows. Christ loved the Church, and showed that love by giving His Blood for her; His whole life here on earth was one of suffering, toil, and pain; and He, as the Head of His Church Militant, was a man of sorrows, and acquainted with grief. But as it was with Him, so must it be with His ministry, His agents, His representatives. To them hath He bequeathed the royal heritage of sorrow. He hath appointed unto them to endure afflictions, even to the end; and so must it be, while the Church is yet in her first condition, tossed on the seas of this life. To the Apostles, therefore, there remained, in trust as it were, good store of trial, pain, and grief, "of Christ," i. e., appointed by Him, and imposed on them by Him; which they must "fill up," i. e., endure, sustain, improve to the full, until the end; afflictions in the flesh, in persecutions, in privations, in peril, yea, in mortification, self-discipline, self-conquest; all to be borne, in faith, in patience, in heavenly joy, that Christ might thereby be glorified.

But Saint Leo gives another explanation. Remarking, that when Saul, the persecutor of the infant Church, was met by the Lord on the way to Damascus, that Lord demanded of him, "why persecutest thou Me?" the holy father says, that since Christ and His Mystical Body are One, therefore injuries done to the Church are injuries also to Him. And therefore the sufferings of the Church, or of the Apostles of the Lord, or of the faithful who believe in Him, are "sufferings of Christ" Himself; since He and His members are one. This interpretation gives the simplest and most natural sense to the words in which resides the main difficulty.

But, howsoever we may take it, one thing is clear: that even as He suffered here on earth, so, while in the way of the journey, must His Church likewise suffer. The life in Christ is a life of trial, temptation, affliction; and they may count themselves especially blessed and favored, who, in the way of the Cross, are made most like unto Him.

"For His Body's sake, which is the Church." "The Mystical Body of Christ;" this is the familiar and characteristic title of the Catholic Church. Her existence, and the mode and manner thereof, are subjects of Faith rather than of sight: "I believe One Holy Catholic and Apostolic Church." And yet men talk of the Church as though she were a society of human origin, and one which we may modify and fashion as we choose. But the Church is divine, as well in respect of her outward and visible form, as in regard to her inner spirit and soul; and no man may without sacrilege make any change in either. She is called the Body of Christ, as being that wherein Christ still dwells here on earth, by His Spirit, after a mystical way, above the power of thought or language to explain or declare.

25. "According," &c. The Apostle no doubt refers to his having been intrusted with the work of preaching this Gospel to the Gentiles. The "dispensation" is the appointment,

25. Whereof I am made a minister, according to the dispensation of God which is given to me for you.

to fulfil the word of
God;

the designation of him; "to you,"
i. e., to you Colossians, to you Laodiceans, to you Gentiles in general.

"To fulfil the word of God." *i. e.*, to aid towards the accomplishment of the Divine promises of ancient time; the prophecies of the past, and the plighted faith and word of the Lord, comprehending universal blessing in the latter days.

26. *Even the mystery which hath been hid from ages and from generations, but now is made manifest to his saints:*

26. "The mystery." Under this term he refers to the whole marvellous work of redemption in Christ. We do not by any means see or comprehend its limits and extent. The Apostle speaks of it, elsewhere, as the Eternal Purpose of God.

"Hid from ages." The reference is to the past days, in which they walked especially by faith, "not having received the promises, but having seen them afar off." For the patriarchs and prophets of the former time knew but little of the designs of the Almighty.

"To His Saints." *i. e.*, to the Church; or it may be, to the Holy Angels, and to the Servants of God in Heavenly Places; for, as the plans of the Lord are carried on towards their fulfilment, they are made more widely and generally known, and the light grows. Perchance, the appearances of the angels, at the time of our Lord's Birth, and, subsequently, during His Life here on earth, and at the time of His Resurrection and Ascension, may be connected with some revelation to them of the manner of that mystery which had been previously wrapped in the secret counsels of the past, and up to the time of our Lord's advent unknown, beyond the Divine sphere.

27. *To whom God would make known what is the riches of the glory of this mystery among the Gentiles; which is Christ in you, the hope of glory:*

27. And now we come to a marvellous statement, of the sum and substance of it all: to what the Apostle calls "the riches of the glory of this mystery;" an expression, in itself, very full and very deep; as though he had said, "this rich and glorious mystery," this mystery glorious in the wealth of its abundant excellence and goodness. "Among the Gentiles:" for in them, and towards them, was it fulfilled, after the prophecies to that effect. Let us then see how

it is expressed. " Christ in you, the hope of glory." A phrase which divides itself triply, thus :—

1. Christ (objectively).
2. Christ in you (subjectively).
3. Christ, the hope of glory (as well objectively as subjectively).

I remark as follows, upon this culmination of all sublime statements relating to our redemption.

1. CHRIST. Objectively; considered as to the Glory of His Eternal Person ; as incarnate ; as the Word made Flesh, and dwelling among us, full of grace and truth ; as God manifest through the veil of the Humanity which He assumed. As sublime in His mortal course; without blemish and without spot; perfect and sinless. As the Exemplar of the highest and best life. As lifted on the Cross, the symbol of infinite compassion and love. This constitutes a first part of that rich and glorious mystery. And all this was made manifest to the Spirits and Angels above, though revealed but dimly and imperfectly to the prophets and patriarchs who went before.

2. CHRIST IN US. Christ, subjectively considered. As mystically dwelling in all the faithful. As He in whom we are planted by Baptism; in whom we grow by feeding on His Body and Blood. As the Head, whereof we are the members. As the First Born of many brethren. As the Light of the World, and as He that illuminateth every man that cometh into this world. As the Vine, while we are the branches. As entering into the line of Adam's race, and so becoming the source and fountain of a new life to all mankind ; as the Second Adam, in whom all we are made alive. Thus, while we trace and ascribe all wisdom, righteousness, sanctification, and redemption to Him; and find in Him the source and origin of all and any good in us; the name becomes synonymous with wealth, glory, and mystery, to all sorts and conditions of men.

3. CHRIST, IN US, THE HOPE OF GLORY. He, the Only-Begotten of the Father, full of grace and truth ; and summing up in His Person all that is ours, and all of us ; next to be considered, as risen from the dead, ascended into Heaven, and gone up to glory ; whither he had borne up, and carried with him, this our human nature, setting it far above all heavens. For, in Christ, is Man made like unto

the Most High. And what He so glorified, He glorified not for His sake but for ours. Since it was not possible that He, as to His Person, could receive any exaltation, addition, or increase (for that He was eternally God of God, Light of Light, Very God of Very God); it follows, that all was done for us, and that He exalted, not Himself, but that nature which He had assumed. And therefore He said, "the Glory which Thou gavest Me, I have given them." He is therefore our "hope;" the "hope of glory," to us; for since He hath so glorified this common nature of ours, we hope to receive of His Hand, hereafter, according to our measure and capacity. And so, the whole creation waiteth for the manifestation of the Sons of God; which shall take place at the last; which in His times He shall show who is the Blessed and Only Potentate, the King of kings and Lord of lords, "*Rex regum et Dominus dominantium;*" which shall come to pass, when this corruptible shall have put on incorruption, and this mortal shall have put on immortality; at the hour of the Resurrection of the Flesh, yea of all flesh; when Death shall be swallowed up in victory, and when the kingdoms of this world shall become the kingdoms of the Lord and of His Christ, and He shall reign forever and ever.

This is "THE RICHES OF THE GLORY OF THIS MYSTERY."

And note, expressly, that the knowledge of all this is to be "among the Gentiles." That is to say, everywhere, and to all the ends of the earth. For the plan embraces all; and is, and must be, effectual towards all who will receive and hold and live therein. See Psalm xcvi., the prophecy, in song, of this glorious mystery; every syllable of which may be applied to these words of Saint Paul. And, therefore, we will set this as a triumphal hymn, after those words, and call it:—

THE SONG OF THE WHOLE EARTH UNTO CHRIST.

1. O sing unto the LORD a new song; sing unto the LORD, all the whole earth.

2. Sing unto the LORD, and praise His Name; be telling of His salvation from day to day.

2. Declare His honour unto the heathen, and His wonders unto all people.

4. For the LORD is great and cannot worthily be praised; He is more to be feared than all gods.

5. As for all the gods of the heathen, they are

but idols; but it is the LORD that made the heavens.

6. Glory and worship are before Him; power and honour are in His sanctuary.

7. Ascribe unto the LORD, O ye kindreds of the people, ascribe unto the LORD worship and power.

8. Ascribe unto the LORD the honour due unto His Name; bring presents, and come into His courts.

9. O worship the LORD in the beauty of holiness: let the whole earth stand in awe of Him.

10. Tell it out among the heathen, that the LORD is King: and that it is He who hath made the round world so fast that it cannot be moved; and how that He shall judge the people righteously.

11. Let the heavens rejoice, and let the earth be glad; let the sea make a noise, and all that therein is.

12. Let the field* be joyful, and all that is in it: then shall all the trees of the wood rejoice before the LORD.

13. For He cometh, for He cometh to judge the earth: and with righteousness to judge the world, and the people with His truth.

28. Whom we preach, warning every man, and teaching every man in all wisdom; that we may present every man perfect in Christ Jesus:

28. "Warning every man," who is in ignorance and sin.

"Teaching every man," who will yield himself to the apostolic guidance.

"In all wisdom;" unto the fulness of spiritual knowledge, and the comprehending with all saints what is the length and breadth and depth and height of the divine and transcendent theme.

29. Whereunto I also labour, striving according to his working, which worketh in me mightily.

29. Note in this verse, the human and the divine power, how they are at once united and contrasted. The man works; but only so as to work "according to God;" and it is GOD that worketh in him mightily. What is said here, of the apostolic power, is also true, in its proper sphere, of the inner work in all separate souls unto salvation and eternal life. We continue at once, to the next chapter.

---

* "The field is the world." S. Matt. xiii. 38.

(CHAPTER II.)

1. For I would that ye knew what great conflict I have for you, and *for* them at Laodicea, and *for* as many as have not seen my face in the flesh;

1. "For." This word connects with the preceding verse: the labors and strife of the Apostle are due to his intense solicitude for them.

"Conflict," to wit, of the spirit and soul. God only knoweth what they suffer, who in addition to a sensitive and anxious temper, prone to prognosticate calamity, are charged with the awful work of watching for souls.

It is rightly inferred from this verse, that S. Paul had never visited these regions; that he was, by face, a stranger to them.

2. That their hearts might be comforted, being knit together in love, and unto all riches of the full assurance of understanding, to the acknowledgment of the mystery of God, and of the Father, and of Christ;

2. The end and ground of this solicitude are set forth: it is that the Church, sore troubled in this evil world, might have and enjoy that profound consolation which comes with the full realization of the higher mysteries of the faith, and with brotherly unity and love in the one holy confession.

"And unto all riches," &c. Paraphrase thus: " that they may be held and united together by the bond of charity, so as fully and perfectly to know and be persuaded concerning the mysteries," &c., &c., &c.

"The Mystery of God, and of the Father, and of Christ." Here again we pause, and reverently observe the distinctions of holy doctrine, and the wide range of the apostolic thought. For he speaks:

1st, of the Mystery of God.

2dly, of the Mystery of the Father.

3dly, of the Mystery of Christ, in whom are hid all the treasures of wisdom and knowledge.

To the rightly understanding all these things, we must take as our guide and key, the creed of the Catholic Church; for that key alone can admit to the full view of these solemn splendors, these comforts and consolations of the faithful and of mankind.

1st, then, we must acknowledge the Mystery of God; that is, of the Most Holy and Undivided Trinity, Three Persons in One Substance.

2dly, we are comforted in the full assurance of understanding of the Eternal Father. For the Father is only such in respect of His Eternal Son; and therefore it is in the Eternal Generation of the Son of God, "begotten of His Father before all worlds," that the Church perpetually rejoices.

3dly, we have the riches of the glory of the Mystery of Christ, the Incarnate Word; and, especially, the truth, that in Him, as Man, are hidden all the treasures of wisdom and knowledge. For, although perfect in wisdom, as God, yet was He, as to His Human Soul, imperfect therein; and "He grew in wisdom" as He "grew in stature," even to the fulness of all wisdom and knowledge, and the abundance of the same. Therefore is the Lord Christ a hidden treasure, a treasure hid in the field which is the world, that a man may sell all that he hath and buy it, unto the perpetual enriching of his life.

These are the divine mysteries concerning which the Apostle felt such deep solicitude, that they might be realized by the Church, and dwelt in, and made the substance of everlasting felicity, and the well-spring of joy and gladness to all the people of God.

We need not be surprised to encounter, next, some reference to prevailing heresies, some warning against them. We learn, from the language of the Apostle, 1st, that false teachers had not been absent; 2dly, that they had done, so far, but little harm. There are allusions here, which show that Gnostic and Judaizing preachers had been busily engaged in sowing tares among the wheat.

3. In whom are hid all the treasures of wisdom and knowledge.

4. And this I say, lest any man should beguile you with enticing words.

5. For though I be absent in the flesh, yet am I with you in the spirit, joying and beholding your order, and the stedfastness of your faith in Christ.

6. As ye have therefore received Christ Je-

4. "And this I say."[*] I have said, and insisted on, what has preceded.

5. From this we see that they had successfully resisted the temptation. "Order:" the outward system of the Church; "faith," her inner life.

6. To receive Christ Jesus, is not merely to have heard of Him by the hearing of the ear, but to have been grafted into Him, sacramentally, as afterwards described; to have Him "in us, the hope of glory." This is the outward and objective fact of their position. "Walk ye in Him:"

sus the Lord, *so* walk ye in him:

7. Rooted and built up in him, and stablished in the faith, as ye have been taught, abounding therein with thanksgiving.

this is the end; the logical sequence, according to His will. See remarks on Gal. v. 25.

7. "Rooted," by the holy sacrament, whereby we are made members of His Mystical Body.

"Built up," by the means of grace, and specially by the Communion of His Body and Blood. "Rooted," again, by the first firm faith in Him, whereby we laid hold of Him as the Redeemer: "built up," by love and obedience, realizing Him to us in all the fulness of His sufficiency.

"Stablished in the faith ..." Confirmed and strengthened in the true profession of the Creeds of the Church, with all that they imply, as well internally as externally.

"As ye have been taught ..." for our religion is not one of our own invention or discovery, nor a system of selfwill and choice, but it is that which we have received by the tradition of parents, spiritual pastors, and sponsors.

8. Beware lest any man spoil you through philosophy and vain deceit, after the tradition of men, after the rudiments of the world, and not after Christ.

8. "Philosophy." Doubtless the apostle speaks of the schools of Greece, and of all those systems of invention based on the idea of the sufficiency of the human reason, by which the old world was led to its destruction. At Athens he encountered them, in their strength and pride, and there he preached in vain to men misled by those deceitful schemes. In general this ancient philosophy may be considered under the three heads of—

1. Object.
2. Method.
3. Results.

The object sought was, to acquire certain knowledge respecting God, Man, the Soul, the nature and destiny of our race, the origin of the world, the foundations of moral duty, the laws of society, and the like topics.

The method followed was that of investigation, not of demonstration. Starting on a supposed or pretended basis of absolute ignorance, the ancients sought, by the processes of thought, reflection, and comparison, to arrive at a knowledge of the unknown, and attempted to discover all moral and spiritual truth.

The results were, total discrepancy in their conclusions;

and a general skepticism. The system was faulty in two respects: 1st, it presupposed a basis of total ignorance as the starting point in investigation. But man has never been, and never can be in such a condition, because the traditions of the primal age have nowhere been obliterated. 2dly, it attributed to the human reason a power of acting to advantage independently of any revelation from outside. But the reason, unaided, is as useless as the eye without light; it was so constituted as to act on being externally illuminated, but not otherwise. The old philosophy assigned to the human mind the office, and claimed for it the power, of a purely independent investigator; and men endeavored, by the way of mere intellectual exercise, to arrive at the knowledge of all that should be believed or done. The result was, utter discord in opinions, and final skepticism.

"Vain deceit." These words truly describe the Rationalistic Philosophy, as well in its modern as in its ancient forms.

"After the tradition of men." "*Græci sapientiam quærunt, stulti facti sunt:*" professing themselves wise, they became fools. It is the same story from beginning to end. Look, *e. g.*, at the totally discordant conclusions at which the human mind arrived, when, freer than it ever was before or ever can be again, it launched forth on the voyage of independent inquiry, and thus affected to come at the knowledge of the truth. Let us recall some of these opinions of the old philosophers. 1st, concerning God:—

Anaximander, holding Infinity to be the principle of all things, yet unable to give any clear account of what he meant, considered that the gods are finite, and that they rise and set after long intervals.

Anaximenes held that the Air is God, begotten, immense, infinite, and perpetually in motion.

Xenocrates spoke of two supreme Gods, a male and a female one; and again, of the stars as deities of different ranks and grades.

Polemo held that the World is God, and that there is none else.

Empedocles asserted the existence of four Gods, corresponding to the four elements, viz.: the Heat and Æther, *Jupiter;* the vital Air, *Juno;* the Earth, *Pluto;* and the Water, *Nestis.*

Xenophanes held that God has a figure, and that it is round.

Melissus says, that we ought not to assert any thing concerning the gods, forasmuch as we have not any knowledge of them.

Such are some of the results of Rational Inquiry, untrammelled and free, as to the first and essential theme of knowledge. Now let us see its discoveries concerning the Soul:

Anaxagoras held that the soul is aerial, and has a body of its own of the nature of Air.

Heraclitus held that Fire is the principle of all things; that the World has a Soul, which is an exhalation of the humid parts thereof; and that the human soul is also an exhalation, but that it is found in different degrees of moisture, and that the dryer a soul is the wiser it is, and the better.

Empedocles held a kind of transmutation of the soul, by which it puts on the several forms of all living creatures and plants; saying of himself, that he had been a boy, a maid, a plant, a bird, and a fish swimming in the sea.

Pythagoras, and his school, entertained various opinions on this point, regarding the soul as a fragment or portion of Cold Æther, as they termed it; or as an aggregation of motes in that Æther; or as that which moves those motes. But he says, more particularly, that there is a Soul intent and commeant through the whole nature of things, from which our souls are plucked or torn off.

Aristoxenes regards it as a vibration of the muscles and fibres of the body, similar to that produced by a stringed instrument.

Other philosophers confound it with the blood around the heart, or speak of it as if it were a material fire within us. But it is unnecessary to cite more of these variations.

3dly. As to the end of human existence, they differ as widely as they could have done:—

Zeno considered it to be Indifference; Callisthenes, Freedom from pain; Aristippus, the pursuit and possession of pleasurable objects; Epicurus, sensual lust, and the satisfying of the fleshly appetites; Aristotle, the delights of the Intellect; Pyrrho, apathy; Theophrastus,

the attainment of riches; Herillus, growth in knowledge, &c., &c., &c.

These were the fruits of speculation about those primary
truths, God, the Soul, and the Chief End of Man. Never
was the Reason better able to show what it could do if
left to itself. Standing between the Past Age and the
Latter Days; having lost the early tradition almost
entirely, and having not yet been enlightened by the
Teaching of the Incarnate Son of God; it was really
in a state of almost complete independence, and able to
assert and exercise its far-famed powers. It did so. And
the result was a demonstration, good for all time, that the
Reason is utterly helpless without revelation, and cannot
arrive, in the exercise of its own resources, at any certain
knowledge on those subjects on which to be uncertain is
to be inexpressibly miserable, weak, and destitute. The
whole system of the Ancient Philosophy, the legitimate
child of the Fallen Intellect, was an enormous failure, and,
in the Apostle's time, a putrefying carcass. These were
the "rudiments of the world;" and this was their value
to mankind.

"And not after Christ." The Apostle places Christ in
opposition to the "philosophy" of the ancients; as though
the Lord were the corrective and the antidote to that
"vain deceit." Compare also the opening chapter of the
first Epistle to the Corinthians. And, indeed, it is true of
all the modern systems of intellectual philosophy, as those
of Germany and France more particularly, that they are
utterly foreign to the Religion of Christ. The Philoso-
phies of Europe, the Cartesian and Leibnitzian; the Spino-
sism and Hegelianism of Germany; the Parkerism and
Transcendentalism of our own day; all alike are but
"vain deceit." It may be said with truth of their authors
and scholars, as of the Greeks, "sapientiam quærunt,
stulti facti sunt." The Creeds of the Catholic Church are
the standing test of all philosophy: what agrees with them
is so far forth truth; what differs from them, or cannot be
harmonized with them, is folly.

9, 10. Here is the Apostolic definition against the philosophism of his
times; and this language do we also
adopt as against all the so-called wisdom of our own day. Observe the

9. For in him dwell-
eth all the fulness of
the Godhead bodily.

10. And ye are com-
plete in him, which is

the head of all princi- correspondence of these statements,
pality and power: which in fact need each other :—

1. In Christ dwelleth all the fulness of the Godhead.

2. Man is complete and perfect, in Him.

The starting point and first principle of Rationalistic
Philosophy, in all times, as well in France, Germany,
England, and New England, of the 17th, 18th, and 19th
centuries, as in Greece and Italy of the centuries succeed-
ing and following the First Advent, is this: That the
Human Reason is able of itself, and in the exercise of its
native powers, and without aid from any quarter, to arrive
at the knowledge of spiritual and ethical truth; that in
all philosophic studies, the mind should set out in a condition of entire ignorance ; that it shall proceed from the
unknown to the known; that it is to find out for itself
whatever shall be regarded as true; and that nothing
should be held as true which has not been thus attained.
The base is always taken within the man ; in his mind,
his intellectual operations, his soul. And thus, different
schools have chosen as the criterion, Consciousness, or
Evidence, or the Pure Reason, or the Logical Faculty, or
Intuition, or the Moral Sense. But the whole process is
earthy, and smells of the earth.

The Catholic Religion, however, which is the mother of
all true, sound, and valuable philosophy, teaches :—

1st, That in the Incarnate Son of GOD dwells all the
fulness of the Godhead ; and that He as Man is the Fountain, Source, and Cause of all wisdom, skill, knowledge,
and power.

2dly, That, by the force of institutions and rites mirac-
ulously potent to that end, men are so grafted into Him,
that His life and their life are identified; that His wisdom
becomes theirs, His knowledge theirs, His strength, power,
righteousness, theirs. Thus they are complete in Him.
And there can be no completeness in them apart from
Him : nor any approach towards it. So that, as regards
the Knowledge of GOD, of ourselves, of the soul, of our
duty, of our destiny, we have no clue out of Christ ; but
in Him all these things may be known, so far as it is permitted us in our present state to know them. In Him are
hid all the treasures of wisdom and knowledge ; and
through Him only have we access thereto. While the
philosophism, of this or any time, which seeks to make

men wiser and better, apart from, and without reference to Christ, is but insane trifling, and a fruitless stock of lies. And above the writings of all the philosophic schools, whether ancient or modern, we inscribe forever the Apostolic description :—

"*Clouds they are without water, carried about of winds; trees whose fruit withereth, without fruit, twice dead, plucked up by the roots; raging waves of the sea foaming out their own shame; wandering stars, to whom is reserved the blackness of darkness forever.*"

9. "In Him :" *i. e.*, in Christ.

"Dwelleth :" perpetually ; see Art. II. The Human and the Divine in His Person are never to be divided ; but He is God-man forever and ever.

"All the fulness of the Godhead." Full deity, with all its perfections and attributes ; and consequently all wisdom and knowledge.

"Bodily." As the soul inhabits the body, in man ; truly, really, and substantially, and not as in a shadow ; in Him, as very Man, true Body, and true Soul ; by a twofold Union ; viz., by a spiritual union between Christ's Human Soul and the word of GOD, and by a corporal union between Christ's Human Body, and the same Divine Person.

Mystery of Mysteries ! Who shall declare His Generation, or his Manner of Life !

Therefore let none be heard, but He. And let all human wisdom be counted folly and loss, except it express the Truth as it is in Him.

10. "And ye are complete in Him." Ye are filled, replenished, with and by His fulness, each according to his measure, in wisdom, knowledge, and all spiritual gifts.

"Who is the head," &c. Who is no creature, but far above all the angelic hosts and orders ; the Head and Lord of all the Thrones, Dominations, Princeships, and Powers, as their Creator.

11. In whom also ye are circumcised with the circumcision made without hands, in putting off the body of the sins of the flesh by the circumcision of Christ:

11. As the Apostle has referred to the heathen systems of philosophy, so now does he correct Jewish error.

"Circumcised." The true circumcision is not that of the Law of Moses, but the circumcision of the heart; the spiritual work of the Holy Ghost. Intending to speak of Holy Baptism, he refers to the rite of Jewish initiation, as a type.

" Made without hands." For it is the work of the Spirit of GOD.

" In putting off," &c. As the ancient rite removed a portion of the flesh, so doth the Holy Ghost cast away and destroy the old body of sin, the body of this death. It is a spiritual circumcision, whereby original sin is pardoned, and its guilt forever removed; whereby the power of sin is broken, and its influence weakened; whereby we are accepted unto sanctification and holiness in the Lord.

" By the circumcision of Christ." By that circumcision which is conferred through Christ, to them that are made His; called " Christ's," as that which He, by the Spirit, performs. " Of Christ," is probably here equivalent to " Christian."

12. Buried with him in baptism, wherein also ye are risen with *him* through the faith of the operation of God, who hath raised him from the dead.

12. "Buried with Him in Baptism." The Instrumental means of our union with Christ. For in that Holy Sacrament we are made members of Him, the Incarnate Saviour; members of His Body, of His Flesh, and of His Bones. This is the great mystery of Christ and the Church : "Magnum sacramentum," as the Vulgate hath it. See remarks on Romans vi. 3, 4. Observe also, that this is an absolute statement; the Apostle asserts that, in baptism, they had been buried with Christ, and were risen again with Him. Therefore, the first word of chap. iii., the hinging word of the epistle, yonder IF, has no doubtful or hypothetical sense, but is equivalent to SINCE.

"Through the faith," &c. The idea is, that the same almighty power which wrought to raise up our Lord from the dead, works still and ever, to produce the mystical and spiritual death and resurrection in holy baptism. That sacrament is therefore no outward rite, no empty form, but the instrument and engine of the vast and wonderworking power of Almighty GOD; and the faith which we must yield is a faith in Him as acting on us thereby. The power comes from without, through that channel; and the evidence to us that it has been exerted and applied, is not in our feelings, but in His word.

8

To exemplify the drift of the human mind averse from God, let it be noted how the modern sect styled Baptists insist on immersion, from the cast of these expressions, while they deny altogether the spiritual power of the rite. They have retained an empty shell. They will hear of no baptism save by immersion : and yet they make of baptism a mere outward rite without spiritual and saving force. This is Materialism and Formalism in the last degree of development.

13. And you, being dead in your sins and the uncircumcision of your flesh, hath he quickened together with him, having forgiven you all trespasses;

13. A continuation of the foregoing statements; a fuller description of the condition of those who are sacramentally in Christ, and He in them.

"Being dead in sins." Reference is to our original state as fallen sinners.

"The uncircumcision," &c., i. e., in the guilt and misery of the natural condition, before the Grace of Christ is given.

"Your flesh." The complete nature, material, spiritual, moral, and intellectual; all disordered and disorganized throughout, by sin.

"Hath He quickened." He, i. e., the Eternal Father.

"Together with Him." Together with Christ; for when the Father did so raise up our Lord from the dead, He brought Him up as the first-fruits ; and we, and all mankind, were potentially raised along with Christ, so as that His Resurrection was, in a manner, that of all mankind.

"Having forgiven you all trespasses." That the sacrament of holy baptism is the appointed instrument for the conferring upon its recipients the pardon of their native guilt, is, with Christians, an article of faith. "I BELIEVE IN ONE BAPTISM FOR THE REMISSION OF SINS." See, also, Acts ii. 38; xxii. 16. It is a sacred mystery, not an intelligible occurrence ; it belongs to the sphere of the miraculous and the divine. Therein have we remission of original sin, once for all, absolutely and unconditionally: and therein have we prospective and promised pardon of all actual sin, what time soever, with true repentance, we ask it of God. These things are *believed*, not understood : they constitute a part of the creed of the faithful soul.

14. Blotting out the handwriting of ordi-

14, 15. We come now to a passage of which Saint Chrysostom thought

nances that was against us, which was contrary to us, and took it out of the way, nailing it to his cross;

15. *And* having spoiled principalities and powers, he made a shew of them openly, triumphing over them in it.

the sublimity to be unsurpassed by any thing in the writings of the Holy Apostle.

There is a certain confusion here. In verses 12, 13, it is the Eternal Father who is mentioned as the Agent. And yet, although the pronoun remains unchanged, and there is hardly any pause, we must understand, in verses 14 and 15, that Christ is spoken of, and that it is He who blotted out the handwriting, who spoiled principalities and powers, &c.

The questions which may be raised about this verse will be resolved according to the meanings which are attached to the words "handwriting" and "ordinances."

1st, then, by the "ordinances" may be understood the precepts and laws of the Mosaic System; and in the word "handwriting" there may be seen a reference to the act of God in writing the commandments upon the two tables of stone, while in its more exact and fuller sense it might be taken as referring to the transcription of the whole code of ceremonies, &c., in the Sacred Books of Israel. That old legal system might properly be referred to, moreover, as being "against" men, since it showed them the guilt of their sins, and the need of expiation, while it left them devoid of any sufficient sacrifice or satisfaction. In this narrow sense, then, the whole passage may be applied to the abrogation of the covenant made through Moses; for when Christ came, it ceased, and was "taken away."

But, 2dly, we make a wider application thus. The word rendered "ordinances," may be regarded as signifying that perpetual Law by which Sin and Death are everlastingly coupled together. "The soul that sinneth, it shall die:" that is a universal ordinance. It is "against" us all, because we have all sinned. And if we take the word in that sense, then the "handwriting" will signify the subscription of each individual sinner to that decree; so that every one, through his particular sins, becomes obnoxious to the general sentence, and signs and sets the seal to his condemnation.

Next, it must be observed that the Apostle speaks of this handwriting and ordinance, as a kind of bond or legal instrument; for it was annulled by the being nailed to the cross. The figure is that of cancelling a bond; and the foregoing explanation enables us at once to apply it.

Lastly, note that in thus cancelling the bond, the Lord is said to have "spoiled principalities and powers, and to have made a shew of them openly." Doubtless the principalities and powers here spoken of are the Devil and his angels. But man, by transgression, fell into the adversary's hand, and became bound to him, and incurred the sentence of death. The Devil, therefore, held him under bondage, and might justly claim the righteous execution of the sentence. When, therefore, the Lord cancels the bond, by striking through it the nails of His cross, He does so "spoil" the Devil, in delivering the sinner out of his hand even as a bird out of the snare of the fowler.

Thus, in a double sense do we make application of this grand passage. 1st, it refers to the old Mosaic System. Our Lord brought that System to an end; He cancelled the old handwriting of ordinances and rites, by executing the functions of the true Priesthood in the midst of the Israel of the old election. And 2dly, it refers to the redemption of all mankind. For Christ, on His cross, put away the old Decree of Condemnation, in offering Himself a full and sufficient sacrifice, in affording to the sinner access to God, and in giving him peace through His Blood. In figure, and substantially, He rent in twain, and, nailing it to the cross-head, cancelled the edict. He annulled, destroyed, and removed forever, the ancient bond of Eternal Death. And thus did He spoil the kingdom of Darkness. For by transgression the First Adam came into bondage unto the Devil. But the Second Adam delivered His brother, and made agreement unto God for him, thereby wresting from the jaws of Hell and Death their prey; yea, He made a show of those powers of darkness openly, leading captive the captivity, and scattering the diabolic hosts, and, before God, angels, and men, triumphing in and by His Cross.

16. Let no man therefore judge you in meat, or in drink, or in respect of an holyday, or of the new moon, or of the sabbath *days.*

16. The Apostle now proceeds to warn them against the influences of those who would seduce them from the faith, and to confirm them in their position, by a comparison of their position, so high and glorious, with the weak inventions of men.

"Let no man therefore judge you." *i. e.*, pay no attention whatever to the remarks of those who find fault with you for not observing the obsolete Jewish rites.

"Meat, drink," &c. He refers to the customs of the Mosaic system. While that system was in force, all these things were of obligation, as commanded by God. But after that system was abrogated, the obligation ceased, and observance of them became self-will and superstition.

17. Which are a shadow of things to come; but the body *is* of Christ.

17. The old system was a type, or symbolic representation of the new. But when Christ came, the types and shadows were done away.

18. Let no man beguile you of your reward in a voluntary humility and worshipping of angels, intruding into those things which he hath not seen, vainly puffed up by his fleshly mind,

18. Other classes of errors are here referred to; such as the Gnostic, a system of angel-worship and creature-worship. For, as the fathers say, there were those who taught that it was too great a condescension for the Word of God to be our Mediator, and that, as in the old system, so in the new, angels were the suitable and true mediators between God and men, and that we ought to have recurrence to them as helpers and intercessors. This was what S. Paul calls the introduction of a superstitious reverence towards angels, accompanied by a feigned and affected humility towards God.

"Vainly puffed up," &c. Not merely is this true of those early heretics who professed full knowledge of the divine mysteries, accurately describing the numbers, nature, names, offices of the angels and heavenly beings, as though the knowledge had been obtained by them from personal inspection. But it is true of Heresy, always and everywhere. All heresy is choice and self-will; the result of independent thought apart from God's revelation. And this is the sign of the fleshly mind, and of the heart that is puffed up with pride and with a sense of its own importance, adequacy, resources, and abilities.

19. And not holding the Head, from which all the body by joints and bands having nourishment ministered, and

19. "Not holding the Head:" *i. e.* Christ. Not holding the true faith concerning Him, His nature, His work: not realizing in practice the confession of the lips. For heresy,

knit together, increaseth with the increase of God.

persisted in, is totally at variance with the spirit of our religion; and the disciples of self-will and those of Christ cannot be the same.

"All the body:" the Catholic Church; of which the Lord is the Head, and whose life is in and from Him.

"Joints and bands:" the figure is carried out in full and with great beauty; these are the ordinances, the sacraments, the means of grace and the channels thereof.

"Nourishment:" the grace of God, which is the very food of the faithful.

"The increase of God:" a divine, a marvellous, a super-human growth; due to the powerful presence of the Almighty, and proving His neighborhood and agency.

20. Wherefore if ye be dead with Christ from the rudiments of the world, why, as though living in the world, are ye subject to ordinances,

20. "Dead with Christ;" dead to human systems, to human inventions; dead to sin and to the world, and the rudiments thereof; dead to the ancient Jewish system, dead to the later philosophic sect-teaching; dead in baptism, dead in the Church, and risen again to a better hope and a better life.

"The rudiments of the world:" it would seem that the Mosaic ordinances are especially intended here; for the Law was our schoolmaster, and it taught to men the rudiments of divine wisdom and knowledge. But there can be little doubt of a reference to the rules and maxims of divers philosophic sects. For these sects exhibited many and fantastic rules; as, for example, the Pythagoreans, who abstained from beans, &c., &c., &c. He therefore includes under the term *Ordinances*, the Mosaic rules, and those of the heathen religions, absolving Christians from their observance.

"As though living in the world." The Church is in the world, but not of it; and in the manner of their life, her children ought to be marked in difference.

21. (Touch not; taste not; handle not;

21. "Touch not;" a precept applying to meats; "taste not;" a rule for drinks; "handle not," perhaps referring to the arbitrary prohibition of female intercourse and marriage.

22. Which all are to perish with the using;)

22. Paraphrase thus: Which rules concern the transitory and the perish-

after the commandments and doctrines of men? able, and that which, in the very use thereof, passeth away. Rules on such subjects ought not to be held so precious as that the divine mysteries of the Faith should be sacrificed for them.

"After the commandments and doctrines of men." From this we infer that the Apostle was speaking of the heathen philosophic maxims; as his condemnation of them is based on the assertion that they were the order and result of mere individual choice and self-will; while the Mosaic Rites and Customs, even as regarded meats, drinks, purifications, and the like, were the appointment and ordinance of Jehovah. Still, the difficulty will disappear, if we consider that circumstances alter cases. While the Jewish dispensation lasted, those observances were of divine authority, and of obligation. But after Christ's Advent, the Law being fulfilled and abrogated, their authority ceased, and the necessity of observing them existed no more. Then, to impose them afresh, or to endeavor to retain them, was but "will-worship:" it was to require what God had not required, to enjoin what God had disallowed, to seek to raise up what God had permitted to die. Accordingly, those observances should be disregarded, and discarded altogether.

23. Which things have indeed a show of wisdom in will worship, and humility, and neglecting of the body; not in any honour to the satisfying of the flesh.

"Which things." Here the chief reference probably is to the precepts and maxims of the heathen.

"A show of wisdom." It is admitted that bodily discipline is wisdom; and on this principle the penitential system of the Church is founded; for, to mortify the flesh, is the rule of the Christian life. The rites which the Apostle condemns were not then objectionable in principle, but in direction, and as not being connected with that faith from which alone good works can proceed.

"Will-worship, humility," &c., &c. A great zeal in religion, a mortifying of the flesh, a discipline of the body, a denial to the flesh of the satisfaction of its desires, and of an estimation higher than it could rightly claim: all these characteristics appeared in the erroneous systems of the time. They were to be rejected, however, by Christians, because they were not held or enjoined in connection with the system of the Church, and in due subordination to her principles.

In short, this passage teaches us, that the very same things which are "laudable and glorious" if done "in faith," and in reverence for Christ and in obedience to His Church, are useless and wilful when performed after 'the law of a man's own heart and mind. Let no one condemn, absolutely, the things here spoken of, "humility, neglecting of the body," and the withholding from the flesh the honor of full satisfaction of its lusts: for these things belong, pre-eminently, to the system of the Church in saving the soul through discipline of the body. But let him remark that their condemnation by the Apostle is a relative one, in so far as they are part and parcel of foreign systems, and of alien gospels, and are not hallowed by the grace of our Lord, and by the sanction of His delegated authority.

PART SECOND.

THE DUTIES OF THE CHRISTIAN.

CHAPTERS III. AND IV.

PART SECOND

PART SECOND.

In the former part of this epistle, S. Paul has stated, in a manner surprisingly beautiful, the sublime privileges of the Child of God. He has done this, not hypothetically, but absolutely. He has spoken, not of a condition which it was desirable for them to occupy; but of a state in which they had, once for all, been placed. This state he has figuratively described under the significant terms of being dead, buried, and risen again, in Christ our Lord; and he has affirmed of Holy Baptism, that it was the Instrumental Means whereby they had so been united to Christ, and made alive unto God in Him. All these declarations are made positively and without reserve. The Apostle has not spoken of their own efforts, as auxiliary towards the blessed change which had been wrought in them; nor has he mentioned internal evidence, such as feelings, sentiments, or emotions, as constituting to them the proof that they were in a state of salvation. The gift was imparted by an outward ordinance; and the fact that they had received that ordinance was the evidence that the gift was theirs.

And now follows a change of language. The Apostle proceeds to enforce all the duties of a godly, righteous, and sober life. But how, or on what ground, does he thus address them? Simply on the ground of what he has declared. He builds upon a Fact. He assumes that fact to be known, and to have been duly weighed by every one. In the light of that Fact, he regards, and declares, their duty. He argues from it, as from an incontrovertible premiss. He does not, therefore, urge them to become somewhat which they were not then. He does not treat them as yet needing a conversion, or a change of heart;

nor does he hint that they have to become Christians, nor
refer their condition as Christians to any such experience
in the past. But, on the contrary, he exhorts all classes
and conditions and ages,—children, too, as well as adults,
—to an abstinence from sin, from vice, from evil, because
they had received the Gift of God His language implies
a work to be done; the work of setting the affections on
things above, of withdrawing from the world, of mortifying the lusts of the flesh, of declining from sin, of walking
with God; and all this, not as a means of becoming Christians, but as an obligation arising from the fact, that
through baptism, they were Christians already. It is
impossible to exaggerate the importance of this colloca-
tion; of this parallel between the Gift and the Work to
be done, between the Life and the Walk, between the
State and its correlative duties.

All this is realized to us in the system of the Prayer-
book. It has evidently been framed after this model.
Every baptized infant is held to be undoubtedly regenerate in that sacrament. Every child, as soon as it is able
to learn, is taught (or should be taught) that in its baptism
it was made a member of Christ, the Child of God, and an
inheritor of the Kingdom of Heaven. Every child is told
that it is in a state of salvation, because of being a baptized child of the Church, and bidden heartily to thank
the Heavenly Father that this is so. Every child is taught
that it must believe and do as its sponsors promised. Every
child is to be trained to look back to holy baptism as having fixed its state, its belief, its duties. Every child is instructed that it has no more to do, save by holy obedience,
to continue in its actual state, until its life's end. This is
the system of the Church; and this is a practical application of the apostolic principles expressed or implied in this
epistle.

On the other hand, the Popular Religionism of the day
reverses this order, and has introduced thereby another
gospel. It teaches the child, that he is not yet, although
baptized, a child of God. He must look forward to conversion and a change of heart before he dare consider himself in a state of grace. He must try to be good; he must
seek Christ; he must renounce the world; in order that
he may become a Christian. If he feel or seem to be
moved towards these things, it is regarded as a hopeful

sign, auguring favorably of the ultimate result. When he has gone through some great experience, when he has fought some great spiritual battle, then he may find acceptance. It is to subjective processes that his attention is directed; he is told that he must become a Christian; and the evidence of the change, when that change shall have occurred, will be found in his consciousness, and not in any rite or ceremony as instrumental towards the result. This is the scheme of the Popular Religionism of the period: and it is diametrically opposed to the idea of Saint Paul. He looks to the Past, and builds thereon a Present. But this modern system agonizes through its Present towards a Future. He, from the gift already assured, deduces the claim on further grace, and the law of life. But the apostles of the later gospel (if it be permitted so to style what is but a human conceit) expose a present nakedness and misery as a motive to obtaining a relief and deliverance in the future.

In illustration of these thoughts, let the text be carefully studied.

1. If ye then be risen with Christ, seek those things which are above, where Christ sitteth on the right hand of God. 1. "If." This word is the hinge on which the two parts of the Epistle turn. It is the central word, the all-important one. It is not a hypothetical "if;" it expresses no doubt, no uncertainty. For he has just said (ii. 12) that they *were* risen with Christ: it is to that statement and affirmation that the words,—the very same that he had just used,—refer. "If" is equivalent to "since then," or "seeing, therefore, that." And the words, "If ye then be risen with Christ," are equivalent to: "Since then, as I have just said, ye are risen with Christ in baptism."

"Seek those things," &c. Lift up your heads; renounce this world, its lusts, its dreams; and live for a better world to come. Do this BECAUSE ye are already mystically risen with the Lord. Observe that the Apostle does not say, in the modern manner,"Because ye seek those things which are above, therefore ye are, or shall become Christians;" but, "because ye have been made Christians, therefore seek the things of Christ."

2. Set your affection on things above, not on things on the earth. "For," *i. e.* because. Verse 3 contains the reason for doing the thing enjoined in verse 2. It is not "be-

3. For ye are dead, and your life is hid with Christ in God. cause ye set your affection on things above, therefore your life is hid with Christ in God." But, it is the very opposite: "Because ye are dead, and because ye have the germ and seed of the new life; therefore, set your affection on heaven."

"Things above," includes all holy and heavenly mysteries, works, duties, in the Church, although she still be militant here on earth. Her ways are God's way; and her things are the powers of the world to come.

"Dead:" see again verses 11–14 of the preceding chapter. The words express a spiritual state in which, by baptism, they had been placed.

"Your life is hid with Christ in God." A mystical expression, only to be understood in connection with those expressions whereby Christ, in His Human Nature, is described as most intimately allied to the human race. He hath our flesh. We are members of His Body, of His Flesh, and of His Bones. His Resurrection is ours also. In the Tabernacle of His Glorified Nature, is all human nature wrapped up; and as our hope is in Him, and as our help, and strength, and power are in Him; so, after a wonderful way, are we in Him and He in us, His Body and Blood are eaten and received by us, and our life, in the spirit, is in Him, and hidden from human exploration and from mortal ken. This expression, and similar ones, touch the deepest depths of the subject of the Incarnation: God help us to deal with them most reverently.

4. When Christ, *who is* our life, shall appear, then shall ye also appear with him in glory.

5. Mortify therefore your members which are upon the earth; fornication, uncleanness, inordinate affection, evil concupiscence, and covetousness, which is idolatry:

Observe again the order of the thought: it is determined by the "therefore" in verse 5. They are to mortify the flesh with the affections and lusts thereof, *because* they are destined to appear with the Lord in glory. How strangely must this sequence sound to modern ears! For the language would have to be reversed to fit the theories of this day; and it should read; "by mortifying your members which are upon the earth, you will become so changed as to be fit to appear with the Lord in glory." But this is not at all the current of the apostolic thought. They have the promise already, the right, the privilege, the expectation : *therefore*, they are to abstain from the lusts of the flesh here enumerated.

"Covetousness, which is idolatry." For self is the centre of covetousness, and thus God's place is usurped. It is the sin of Balaam and of Judas which is here spoken of; a sin whose punishment has been slow, but sure and fearful.

6. For which things' sake the wrath of God cometh on the children of disobedience :

6. The unconverted and ungodly are meant; those who are not yet in a state of grace and salvation.

7. In the which ye also walked some time, when ye lived in them.

7. Note here the difference between "walked" and "lived." To live in those things, was, to be in the natural condition of the fallen creature; unpardoned, unaccepted, without power. They "walked" in such sins, *i. e.* committed them when they "lived" in that their native and unregenerate condition.

8. But now ye also put off all these; anger, wrath, malice, blasphemy, filthy communication out of your mouth.
9. Lie not one to another, seeing that ye have put off the old man with his deeds;
10. And have put on the new *man*, which is renewed in knowledge after the image of him that created him :

8. Take this verse with the next, and note again the order of the thought. Anger, wrath, blasphemy, lies, and the like, are to be put off, because the old nature has been put off, and the new put on. Observe especially, that he says, that they *have* put off the old man and put on the new : that much is settled ; that is a fixed fact. But remark also, that the putting off anger, wrath, malice, &c., is enjoined as a work to be done, even by them. How different from the popular scheme ! in which, the exhortation is to get Christ, to come to Christ, to put on Christ. According to modern notions, the thing to be done is to put on Christ, and the way to this result is to put off the old man with his deeds. But according to the old and primitive idea, Christ has been put on already by all the baptized, and that is the motive to stifling the remnants of sin.

"The old man :" the sinful, corrupt, and fallen nature wherein we were all conceived and born. Into this is the seed and germ of the new life inserted by the power of our Lord and the co-operation of the Holy Ghost.

"The new man :" the regenerate nature, the nature made

alive to hope, and joy, and love, through our Lord, and through the power of His Holy Spirit.

Observe upon these verses, that by "the old man" and "the new man," are not meant the First Adam and the Second Adam. For although it is customary with the Apostle to speak of putting on Christ, yet we nowhere find such an expression as, putting off Adam. Therefore the words, "put on the new man," cannot here mean putting on Christ; because there must be a correspondence between the two clauses, and they could only have that sense if the former phrase, "put off the old man," meant putting off Adam, which expression is incongruous and inadmissible. Since then two persons are not meant, the expression must be taken as denoting two different states of the same individual. The old man, is the nature in its original condition; the new man, is that nature in its regenerate state.

Again observe, that these expressions relate, not to the individual character, but to the common nature. In other words, to put off the old man, does not mean to cease from sinning and to do righteousness. To take it in that sense, would be to represent S. Paul as an illogical thinker and a careless writer. For this absurd tautology would follow, if we paraphrased the verses: "Put off anger, wrath, malice, blasphemy, &c.; lie not one to another; follow a pure morality, lead godly lives; because ye have already put away anger, wrath, &c., because ye do not lie any more, because ye are leading godly lives." In short, he who attentively considers these verses cannot fail to perceive, that to put off the old man is one thing, and to put off the habits of anger, malice, blasphemy, lying, &c., is another and a different thing. The latter is that to which they are exhorted; the former is that which has already occurred. *Because* they have put off the old man and put on the new, *therefore* they ought to put off and to put aside all habits and acts of sinfulness. This is the whole sum and substance of the Catholic Philosophy of Life. Nature and character are not the same. Nature is the field of God's operation; character is the result of man's activity. Nature is that whereto the holy sacraments are applied; character is the result of man's co-operation with or despising of grace. To put off malice, anger, blasphemy, &c., is to change the character; to put off the old man and put on the new, is to have and receive a spiritual gift into the deep nature, even the inner and hidden part of this marvellous being. Without these distinctions, the words of the Apostle must ever seem confused, illogical, and obscure; he but repeats himself, and rambles babbling. But with these distinctions kept in view, his words are wonderfully profound and comprehensive, and we hear in them as it were the voice of the God of the spirits of all flesh; of Him who assumed, not any individual's person or character, but the common humanity of all mankind; in whom that nature (and not any one individual) is glorified and exalted forevermore.

"The new man." Compare 2 Cor. v. 17. The regenerated humanity.

"Renewed." Brought back again to a state like that in which our first parents were before the Fall.

"In knowledge." In the clearer knowledge of God and of His will, and of our duties; for in knowledge of Him standeth our eternal life. And see the commentary on Romans i. 20–32.

"After the Image," &c. We were made in the Image of God; Gen. i. 26, 27. That Image was obscured by the Fall. To that Image we are restored, by Grace, through Christ. Therefore the regeneration of the sinner in Holy Baptism is called the new creation; and the sinner a new creature. This, also, the Symbolism of the Church displays; for the Font is made octagonal, in sign of the seven days of the First Creation, and of the added eighth day of the new.

11. Where there is neither Greek nor Jew, circumcision nor uncircumcision, Barbarian, Scythian, bond nor free : but Christ is all, and in all.

11. This statement of the abolishing of all arbitrary distinctions among men, and of the reducing all to obedience to Christ as the Source of Wisdom, Righteousness, Sanctification, and Redemption, follows appropriately upon what has been said thus far as against Greek Philosophy and Jewish Superstition. The thought is this: that there is no power or value in aught that is of man, save in so far as the Lord's Presence may consecrate it for its just and proper use. *Christ is all:* all that we need, all that we can desire, all to man. And *Christ is in all:* indwelling, by His Spirit, so as that our life, our hope, our strength, are in Him. He who

9

would be aught without Christ, feeds on a vain hope. He who would depend on his own light and strength, while Christ dwelleth in Him, profanes that Sacred Presence, and drives the Holy Spirit from beneath his roof.

12. Put on therefore, as the elect of God, holy and beloved, bowels of mercies, kindness, humbleness of mind, meekness, longsuffering;

13. Forbearing one another, and forgiving one another, if any man have a quarrel against any: even as Christ forgave you, so also *do* ye.

14. And above all these things *put on* charity, which is the bond of perfectness.

12. Upon verses 12 and 13, this remark only needs to be made; that all the exhortations contained in them, are based upon the fact of the relation of the parties addressed to Almighty God. They are already His Elect, members of His Church, and, as such, "holy and beloved," sanctified by the Holy Ghost, and beloved in Christ as the many brethren of the First-born.

14. No one ever wrote so beautifully of Charity, of Eternal Love, as this Apostle. See 1 Cor. xiii.; that hymn of Divine Love, than which no sweeter strain was ever sung. Charity is the first and greatest of all; the chief of theological virtues; the life of the world; the very essence of God. The Cross displayed it to all the world; and in the Holy Eucharist it is symbolized and enjoyed perpetually, until the End come. "The bond of Perfection;" for it embraces and connects all virtues, and unites the faithful to each other and to God.

15. And let the peace of God rule in your hearts, to the which also ye are called in one body; and be ye thankful.

15. The vocation of Christians, in the Church, is a vocation unto peace; and in that peace they are to be thankful with exceeding joy.

"Rule in your hearts." There are two senses in which the Greek word here translated "rule" may be understood; an active and a passive. Actively, the idea is that of triumphing victoriously; and then the idea would be, that, over wrath, anger, hatred, lust, &c., the Peace of God should triumph and reign supreme, subduing the whole nature to the Law of Christ. But, in a passive sense, the idea is, that of being bestowed as a prize; and then the thought would be, that, after the trial and hard conflict against the world, the flesh, and the devil, they should receive at the Lord's Hand His good and perfect gift; as it is said,

"Thou wilt keep him in perfect peace, whose mind is stayed on Thee, because he trusteth in Thee."

16. "The word of Christ:" the doc-

16. Let the word of Christ dwell in you richly in all wisdom; teaching and admonishing one another in psalms and hymns and spiritual songs, singing with grace in your hearts to the Lord.

trine concerning Him; the true faith of the Church. The word of life, received from its authorized teachers; studied with deep thought and reverence; rejoiced in with praise and thanksgiving to the Lord for all the treasures of wisdom and knowledge which He hath shown to men.

17. And whatsoever ye do in word or deed, do all in the name of the Lord Jesus, giving thanks to God and the Father by him.

17. The final end of all our works must be the glory of God; and unto that end are they to be begun, continued, and ended. So, they are to be in the Name of Christ, and by the strength which He supplies. And when they are accomplished, the glory and praise are to be perpetually ascribed unto the Most High and Undivided Trinity, and to the Almighty Father, by His Only-begotten Son.

In order that this precept be fulfilled, it suffices that all things be referred to the Glory of God in *habit*, though they be not expressly in *act*.

When, therefore, our works are such, that they may result in glory to God as having inspired them, this law is fulfilled: but he who acts contrary to the glory of God and to His commandment, transgresses also this rule.

It were desirable, however, that all our works should be referred, in act, or at least in force and intention, to the glory of Almighty God, in the name of the Lord Jesus Christ, and in reliance on His power and aid. For thus should all become so many praises and acknowledgments of Him.

"Therefore, by Him, with Him, and in Him, do all things.

"By Him, as thy Mediator and High-Priest;

"With Him, as thy Head;

"In Him, in spirit, motives, intentions."

18. Here follows a summary of du-

18. Wives, submit yourselves unto your own husbands, as it is fit in the Lord.

ties: of wives and husbands, of children and parents; of servants and masters; on which catalogue it is un-

19. Husbands, love your wives, and be not bitter against them.

20. Children, obey your parents in all things: for this is well pleasing unto the Lord.

21. Fathers, provoke not your children to anger, lest they be discouraged.

22. Servants, obey in all things your masters according to the flesh; not with eyeservice, as menpleasers; but in singleness of heart, fearing God:

23. And whatsoever ye do, do it heartily, as to the Lord, and not unto men;

24. Knowing that of the Lord ye shall receive the reward of the inheritance: for ye serve the Lord Christ.

25. But he that doeth wrong shall receive for the wrong which he hath done: and there is no respect of persons.

1. Masters, give unto your servants that which is just and equal; knowing that ye also have a Master in heaven.

necessary particularly to enlarge. But let it be observed, that these are the duties of the "Elect of God," of those who are "buried with Christ in baptism, and risen again with Him therein;" and that the basis of all these exhortations is the preceding gift of grace.

19. "Bitter:" i. e., difficult, morose, vexatious in conduct.

21. "Provoke not," &c.: i. e. be not too harsh, too severe; lay not too heavy a burden on them, nor hold and confine them with an unreasonable severity; for this is to discourage them, to make them despondent, to drive them forth to recklessness of life, when they have liberty and are become their own masters.

22. "Masters according to the flesh:" probably heathen masters are meant. Even to them must the servant be in humble subjection. The next three verses are included in the directions for servants; and the first verse of the next chapter ought not to have been dislocated from its proper place.

23. The service is to be rendered cheerfully and with alacrity, as though it were done to the Lord directly; indirectly, it is done to Him, if done in a right spirit.

24. "The reward of the inheritance;" the wages and fulness of joy and praise in the eternal kingdom.

"Give that," &c. Not merely their due wages, but consideration, kindness, and just and equal treatment according to their station and their rights. Nothing can be more admirable than the way in which the duties of servants and masters are thus contrasted, those duties on both sides being referred to the same Lord, with whom there is no respect of persons. Thus, in the doctrine of the Church, concerning Christ, the God-Man, in whose

Person the finite and the infinite are united, have we the solution of all social problems, as between high and low, rich and poor, master and servant, parent and child, husband and wife, &c., &c. The Incarnation is the Central Truth, on which all other truths depend.

2. Continue in prayer, and watch in the same with thanksgiving;

3. Withal praying also for us, that God would open unto us a door of utterance, to speak the mystery of Christ, for which I am also in bonds:

4. That I may make it manifest, as I ought to speak.

5. Walk in wisdom toward them that are without, redeeming the time.

6. Let your speech be alway with grace, seasoned with salt, that ye may know how ye ought to answer every man.

7. All my state shall Tychicus declare unto you, who is a beloved brother, and a faithful minister and fellowservant in the Lord:

8. Whom I have sent unto you for the same purpose, that he might know your estate, and comfort your hearts;

9. With Onesimus, a faithful and beloved brother, who is one of you. They shall make known unto you all things which are done here.

10. Aristarchus my fellowprisoner saluteth you, and Marcus, sister's son to Barnabas, (touch-

2. A general address to the whole body of the faithful at Colossè is now made.

3. "A door of utterance." An opportunity of preaching the great message as before; this is the sole reason why the Apostle desires deliverance from Cæsar's dungeon; not for himself, but for his work's sake.

5. "Them that are without;" viz., the heathen, towards whom a great discretion and forbearance are to be shown; "redeeming the time," taking advantage of every occasion to advance the cause of the Church and of Christ.

6. The speech should be wise and timely, well seasoned, and adapted to each case as necessity and circumstances require.

8. It is implied that he was to return and bring back word to the Apostle of their condition.

9. Onesimus was a slave; and yet the Apostle calls him "brother." Here is the true Christian idea. "Qui in regnum cœlorum primas tenebat, qui fuit coronatus, qui in tertium ascendit cœlum, servos fratres vocat, et conservos: ubi est insania? ubi est arrogantia? Deprimamus omnes fastum, conculcemus arrogantiam."

11. Aristarchus, Marcus, and Justus, three Jews, are spoken of by the Apostle as having been the only fellow-laborers with him, and they are testified to as having comforted and cheered him by their fidelity; it is

ing whom ye received
commandments: if he
come unto you, receive
him;)

11. And Jesus, which
is called Justus. who
are of the circumcision.
These only *are my* fel-
lowworkers unto the
kingdom of God, which
have been a comfort
unto me.

12. Epaphras, who is
one of you, a servant
of Christ, saluteth you,
always labouring fer-
vently for you in pray-
ers, that ye may stand
perfect and complete
in all the will of God.

13. For I bear him
record, that he hath a
great zeal for you, and
them *that are* in Lao-
dicea, and them in Hi-
erapolis.

14. Luke, the beloved
physician, and Demas,
greet you.

15. Salute the breth-
ren which are in Lao-
dicea, and Nymphas,
and the church which
is in his house.

16. And when this
epistle is read among
you, cause that it be
read also in the church
of the Laodiceans; and
that ye likewise read
the *epistle* from Lao-
dicea.

17. And say to Ar-
chippus, Take heed to
the ministry which thou
hast received in the
Lord, that thou fulfil it.

18. The salutation
by the hand of me
Paul. Remember my
bonds. Grace *be* with
you. Amen.

not necessary that we should so con-
strue these verses as to represent the
Apostle as saying, that none but these
had been faithful: the idea is, " these
are the only fellow-laborers of mine
from among the Jews, and these have
comforted me indeed."

12. Epaphras was himself a Colos-
sian.

16. Diverse views have been taken
of this verse. Some think that there
was an Epistle to the Laodiceans, and
that it has been lost; this is an un-
warrantable explanation of the difficulty. Others think that it was an
Epistle written from Laodicea to S.
Paul, in answer to which he had sent
this letter to the Colossians. Others
again, that it was the Epistle now
known in the Church as that to the
Ephesians, which had been intended
equally for Ephesus and Laodicea.
But the uncertainty cannot now be
cleared up. Only, it is incredible that
an inspired letter could have been
lost. God's revelation is not thus
scattered to the idle wind; the word
of the Lord, as well written as un-
written, liveth and abideth forever.

17. Who was Archippus? and why
did he need this warning? We know
not. But it is a warning, which may
impress us the more from its very
mystery. Like that "nameless column with the buried base," hard by
the place of the Apostle's imprisonment in the Forum, the lack of data
to interpret the history gives to that
history a peculiar power.

18. "Remember my bonds." Yea,
holy saint, long since delivered from
those bonds, and entered into thy
rest, surely they are remembered of

¶ Written from Rome to the Colossians by Tychicus and Onesimus.

the Church, as well as of GOD. In those thy bonds, thou didst not murmur nor repine, though shut within the stones of darkness and under the shadow of death; for it was no chance which so did cast thee down to the sides of the pit, but the will of Him whose servants may serve Him as perfectly in solitude as in the throng of life; as well in the desert and in the cell, as in the market-place or the temple. From those chains, thou hadst no other desire to be released, save this, that thou mightest once more fulfil thy ministry received in the Lord, and preach the unsearchable riches of Christ. The Church remembers thy bonds evermore. She gives thanks for them to GOD, commemorating them, and thee in them, with joy. And still, as bound herself, and militant here on earth, she would follow in the way where her Apostles have trodden, gladly enduring affliction and persecution for a season, until the doors of the everlasting kingdom be unfolded, and until the prisoners of hope be released, and until the Lord shall give deliverance to the captive, and all shall enter together into joy, because the rod of the oppressor is broken and his yoke is departed from the children of men, and his burden from off their shoulders, forever and ever.

Lord Jesus Christ,

BY THEE WERE ALL THINGS CREATED, AND BY THEE DO THEY ALL
CONSIST,

AND YET IN THE BODY OF THY FLESH HAST THOU
REDEEMED US,

TRIUMPHING IN THY CROSS.

Image of the Invisible God;

IN US THY IMAGE IS DEFACED AND MARRED:

Brightness of the Glory of the Father;

THE GLORY OF MAN IS AS THE FLOWER OF THE GRASS,

THE GRASS WITHERETH, AND THE FLOWER THEREOF FALLETH AWAY:

Spoiler of Principalities and Powers;

BEHOLD, HE IS AT HAND THAT DOTH BETRAY US,

YEA, ALL THE WAVES AND STORMS ARE GONE OVER US,

AND OUR VOYAGE IS IN THE NIGHT:

LORD, TO WHOM SHALL WE GO BUT TO THEE?

REVIVE THY WORK IN THE MIDST OF THE YEARS;

RESTORE THE BEAUTY WHICH IS GONE FOR VERY TROUBLE,
AND WORN AWAY;

AND SAY TO THE WINDS AND THE SEA,

AND TO EVERY VOICE OF THE OPPRESSOR,

PEACE, BE STILL.

www.ingramcontent.com/pod-product-compliance
Lightning Source LLC
Chambersburg PA
CBHW020747020726
47495CB00008B/2345

* 9 7 8 3 3 3 7 3 8 1 5 5 4 *